THE DEMONATA

WOLF ISLAND

BY DARREN SHAN

LITTLE, BROWN AND COMPANY
New York Boston

Little, Brown and Company

Hachette Book Group
237 Park Avenue, New York, NY 10017
Visit our website at www.lb-teens.com

Little, Brown and Company is a division of Hachette Book Group, Inc.
The Little, Brown name and logo are trademarks of Hachette Book Group, Inc.

First U.S. Hardcover Edition: May 2009
First U.S. Paperback Edition: April 2010
First published in Great Britain by Collins in 2008

ISBN 978-0-316-04890-3 (hc) / ISBN 978-0-316-04881-1 (pb)

10 9 8 7 6 5 4 3 2

RRD-C

Printed in the United States of America

Also in

THE DEMONATA

series:

Lord Loss (Book 1)

Demon Thief (Book 2)

Slawter (Book 3)

Bec (Book 4)

Blood Beast (Book 5)

Demon Apocalypse (Book 6)

Death's Shadow (Book 7)

Dark Calling (Book 9)

Hell's Heroes (Book 10)

✠ ✠ ✠

✠ ✠ ✠

For:

Bas – managing director of Shan Island

OBEs (Order of the Bloody Entrails) to:
Csilla and Gabor – Budapest's best!

Head Lab Technician:
Stella Paskins

Board of Governors:
The Christopher Little Lambs

✠ ✠ ✠

SHADOW PLAY

A FIVE-HEADED demon with the body of a giant earwig bears down on me. I leap high into the air and unleash a paralyzing spell. The demon stiffens, quivers wildly, then collapses. Its brittle legs shatter beneath the weight of its oversized body. Beranabus and Kernel move in on the helpless bug. I follow halfheartedly, stifling a yawn. Just another dull day at the office.

One of the demon's heads looks like a crow, another a vulture, while the rest look like nothing on Earth. It opens its birdlike beak and squirts a thick green liquid. Beranabus ducks swiftly, but the spit catches Kernel's right arm. His flesh bubbles away to the bone. Cursing with more irritation than pain, he uses magic to cleanse his flesh and repair the damage.

"We could do with a bit of help here," Kernel growls as I stroll after them.

"I doubt it," I grunt, but break into a jog, just in case the demon's tougher than we anticipated. Wouldn't want to let the team down.

The earwig unleashes another ball of spit at Beranabus. The elderly magician flicks a hand at the liquid, which rebounds over the demon's heads. It screams with shock and then agony. Kernel, back to full health, freezes the acidic spit before it fries the creature's brains. We want this ugly baby alive.

I leap onto the demon's back. Its shell is slimy beneath my bare feet. Stinks worse than a thousand sweaty armpits. But in this universe that doesn't even begin to approach the boundaries of disgusting. I confronted a demon made of vomit a few months ago. The only way to subdue it was to suck on the strands of puke and sap it of its strength. Yum!

This wasn't a career move. I didn't read a prospectus and go, "Hmm, drinking demon puke . . . I could do that!" Life just led me here. I'm a magician, and if you're born with a power like mine, you tend to get drawn into the war with the Demonata hordes. I fought my destiny for a long time, but now I grudgingly accept it and get on with the job at hand.

The earwig shudders, overcoming my paralyzing spell. It tries to buck me off, but I dig my toes in and drive a fist through the shell. I let magical warmth flood from my fingers. An electric shock crackles through the demon. It squeals, then collapses limply beneath me.

Beranabus and Kernel face the demon's vulture-like head and interrogate it. I stay perched on its back, hand immersed in its gooey flesh, green blood staining my forearm, nose crinkled against the stench.

"What is it?" Beranabus shouts, punching the twisted head, then grabbing the beak. "What's its real name? Where's it from? How powerful is it? What are its plans?" He releases his hold and waits for an answer.

The demon only moans in response. There are thousands of demon languages. I can't speak any, but there are spells you can cast to understand them. I generally don't bother. I'm sure this demon knows no more about the mysterious Shadow than any of the hundreds we've tormented over the last however many months that we've been on this wild goose chase.

The Shadow is the name we've given to a demon of immense power. It's a massive, pitch-black beast, seemingly stitched together out of patches of shadow, with hundreds of snake-like tentacles. Beranabus thinks it's the greatest threat we've ever faced. Lord Loss — an old foe of mine — said the Shadow was going to destroy the world. When a demon master makes a prediction like that, only a fool doesn't take note.

We've been searching for the monster ever since we first encountered it in a cave, on a night when I lost my brother, but saved the world. We've been trying to find out more about it by torturing creatures like this giant earwig. We know the Shadow has assembled an army of demons, promising them the destruction of mankind and even the end of death itself. But we don't know who it is, where it comes from, exactly how powerful it is.

"This is your last chance," Beranabus growls, taking a step back from the earwig. "Tell us what you know or we'll kill you."

The demon makes a series of spluttering noises. Beranabus and Kernel listen attentively while I scratch my neck and yawn again.

"The same old rubbish," Kernel murmurs when the demon finishes.

"Unless it's lying," Beranabus says without any real hope.

The earwig babbles rapidly, panicked.

"Spare you?" Beranabus muses, as if it's a novel idea. "Why should we?"

More squeaks and splutters.

"Very well," Beranabus says after a short pause. "But if you discover something and don't tell us . . ." There's no need for him to finish. The magician is feared in this universe of horrors. The earwig knows the many kinds of hell we could put it through.

I withdraw my hand from the hole in the earwig's shell and jump to the ground. We're in a gloomy realm, no sun in the dark purple sky. The land around us is like a desert. I make my hand hard and jab it into the dry earth, over and over, cleaning the green blood from my skin. Kernel opens a window while I'm doing that. When I'm ready, we step through into the next zone, in search of more demons to pump for information about the elusive, ominous Shadow.

INNER SILENCE

✠ ✠ ✠

SIX demons later, we rest for a while on a deserted asteroid in the blackest depths of demonic space, each of us sheltered by a magical force field that provides oxygen and warmth. Beranabus creates a few balls of light, directing the rays down, shielding us from any passers-by. In this universe you're never safe, even in areas usually devoid of life.

You don't have to sleep, eat, or drink much here, but it helps to rest every so often and recharge your batteries. I haven't been to this spot before, so I go on a stroll in case there's anything worth seeing. We've cut a wild, meandering route through demon territories since I linked up with Beranabus. He's worried that Lord Loss or others of the Shadow's forces are tracking us, so we've kept on the move, hopefully several steps ahead of any pursuers.

The asteroid's as uninteresting as I thought it would be, just pitted rock, not even any unusual formations. I thought this universe was amazing when I first came. The physical laws vary from zone to zone. I've seen mountains floating overhead. A world made of glass. I've been inside the bowels of giant demons. Squashed miniature worlds, killing billions of bacterial demons with a well-placed foot.

I'm not so easily impressed now. It wears you down, the constant weirdness, torturing, killing. Days and demons blur. You can't stop and marvel at wonders all the time. You start to take them for granted. I see a demon the size of a city, with the face of the *Mona Lisa.* Big deal. All I care about is how to kill it.

I'm not scared anymore either. I was the first few demons we fought. The old Grubbs Grady yellow streak shone through and I had to battle hard to stand my ground and not flee like a spineless loser. But fear fades over time. I no longer worry about dying. It's going to happen sooner rather than later — I've accepted that. I don't even give thanks anymore when we scrape through a fierce battle.

But close fights are rare. Most of the demons we target are weak and craven. We don't tackle the stronger beasts, focusing instead on the dregs of the universe. I could defeat most of them single-handed. We always work as a unit, but don't often need to. I've fought thousands of demons, but I could count the number of times my life has been in danger on the fingers of one hand.

Fighting demons and saving the world might sound awesome, but in fact it's a bore. I used to have more excitement on a Friday night at home, watching a juicy horror flick with Bill-E or wrestling with my friend Loch.

✠ ✠ ✠

✠ Kernel's playing with invisible lights when I return. His eyes were stabbed out in Carcery Vale. I thought he'd be blind for life, but you can work all sorts of miracles in this universe. Using magic, he eventually pieced together a new pair. They look a lot like his original set, only the blue's a shade brighter and tiny flickers of different colors play across them all the time.

The flickers are shadows of hidden patches of light. Apparently, the universes are full of them. When a mage or demon opens a window between realms, the mysterious lights cluster together to create the fissure. But only Kernel can see the patches. He can also manipulate them with his hands, allowing him to open windows faster than any other human or demon.

Beranabus was worried that Kernel might not be able to see the lights when he rebuilt his eyes, but actually his vision has improved. He can see patches he never saw before — small, shimmering lights that constantly change shape. He can't control the newly revealed patches. He's spent a lot of time fiddling with them, without any success.

I sit and watch Kernel's hands making shapes in the air. His eyes are focused, his expression intense, like he's under hypnosis. There are goose bumps on his chocolate-colored skin. Beads of sweat roll down his bald head, but turn to steam as they trickle close to his eyes. He freaks me out when he's like this. He doesn't look human.

Of course he's *not* entirely human. Nor am I. We're hosts to an ancient weapon known as the Kah-Gash, which sets us apart from others of our species. Together with Bec — a girl from the past, but returned to life in the present — we have the power to reverse time and, if the legends are to be believed, destroy an entire universe. Coolio!

I'm constantly aware of the Kah-Gash within me. It's a separate part of myself, forever swirling beneath the surface of my skin and thoughts. It used to speak to me but it hasn't said anything since that night in the cave. I often try to question it, to find out more about the weapon's powers and intentions. But the Kah-Gash is keeping quiet. No matter what I say, it doesn't respond.

Maybe if Kernel, Bec, and I experimented as a team, we could unearth its secrets. But Beranabus is wary of uniting us. We couldn't control the Kah-Gash when we first got together. It took a direction of its own. It worked in our favor on that occasion, but he's afraid it might just as easily work against us next time. The old magician has spent more than a thousand years searching for the scattered pieces of the Kah-Gash, but now that he's reassembled them, he's afraid to test the all-destructive weapon.

I miss the voice of the Kah-Gash. I was never truly alone when it was there, and loneliness is something I'm feeling a lot of now. I miss my half-brother, Bill-E, taken from me forever that night in the cave. I miss school, my friends, Loch's sister, Reni. I miss the world, the life I knew, TV, music — even the weather!

But most of all I miss Dervish. My uncle was like a father

to me since my real dad died. In an odd way I love him more than I loved my parents. I took them for granted and assumed they'd always be around. I knew they'd die at some point, but I thought it would be years ahead, when they were old. Having learned my lesson the hard way, I made the most of every day with Dervish, going to bed thankful every night that he was still alive and with me.

I could tell Dervish about the demons, the dullness, the loneliness. He'd listen politely, then make some dry, cutting comment that would make it all seem fine. Time wouldn't drag if I had Dervish to chat with between battles.

I wonder what he's doing, how he's coping without me, how much time has passed in my world. Time operates differently in this universe. Depending on where you are, it can pass slower or quicker than on Earth. Kernel told me that when he first came here with Beranabus, he thought he'd only spent a few weeks, but he returned home to find that seven years had passed.

We've been trying to stick to zones where time passes at the same rate as on Earth, so that we can respond swiftly if there's a large-scale assault or if Bec gets into trouble. But Beranabus is elderly and fuzzy-headed. If not for the emergence of the Shadow, I think he'd have shuffled off after the fight in the cave to see out his last few years in peace and quiet. Kernel has absolute faith in him, but I wouldn't be shocked if we returned to Earth only to find that a hundred years have passed and everyone we knew is pushing up daisies.

As if reacting to my thoughts, Beranabus groans and rolls onto his back. He blinks at the darkness, then lets his eyelids flutter shut, drifting into sleep. His long, shaggy hair is almost fully grey. His old suit is torn in many places, stained with different shades of demon blood. The flower in the top buttonhole of his jacket, which he wears in memory of Bec, is drooping and has shed most of its petals. His skin is wrinkled and splotchy, caked with filth. His toenails are like dirty, jagged claws. Only his hands are clean and carefully kept, as always.

Kernel mutters a frustrated curse.

"No joy?" I ask.

"I can't get near them," he snaps. "They dart away from my touch. I wish I knew what they were. They're bugging the hell out of me."

"Maybe they're illusions," I suggest. "Imaginary blobs of light. The result of a misconnection between your new eyes and your brain."

"No," Kernel growls. "They're real, I'm sure of it. I just don't know what . . ."

He starts fiddling again. He needs to lighten up. It can't be healthy, wasting his time on a load of lights that might not even be real. Not that I've done a lot more than him in my quieter moments. I wish I had a computer, a TV, a CD player. Hell, I'd even read a book — that's how low I've sunk!

I'm thinking of asking Kernel to open a window back to Earth, so I can nip through and pick up something to distract me, when Beranabus stirs again.

"Was I asleep for long?" he asks.

"A few minutes," I tell him.

He scowls. "I thought I'd been out for hours. That's the

trouble with this damn universe — you can't get any decent sleep."

Beranabus stands and stretches. He looks around with his small, blue-grey eyes and yawns. This is about the only time you can see his mouth properly. Mostly it's hidden behind a thick, bushy beard. All our hair was burnt away when we traveled through time, but it's grown back. I think he looked better without the beard, but he likes it. I grew my red hair the same way as before too. I guess you always go with what you're used to.

"I suppose we'd better —," Beranabus begins.

"Quiet!" Kernel hisses, cocking his head. This is a new tic of his. Several times recently he's shushed us. He says he can hear muted whispers, hints of sounds that seem to come from the patches of light.

A few minutes pass. Kernel listens intently while Beranabus and I keep our peace. Finally he relaxes and shakes his head.

"Could you make out anything?" Beranabus asks.

"No," Kernel sighs. "I'm not even sure it's speech. Maybe it's just white noise."

"Or maybe you're going crazy," I throw in.

"Maybe," Kernel agrees.

"I was joking," I tell him.

"I wasn't," he replies.

"Well, whatever it is, it can wait," Beranabus says. "We've had enough rest. Open another window and we'll go find a few more demons."

Kernel sighs, then concentrates. Roll on the next round of inquisitions and torture.

TO THE RESCUE

✠ ✠ ✠

WE'RE chasing a flock of terrified sheep demons. Each one is covered with hundreds of small, woolly heads. No eyes or ears, just big mouths full of sharp demon teeth. All the better to eat you with, my dear.

Beranabus thinks the sheep might know something about the Shadow. Stronger demons prey on these weak creatures. He's hoping they might have heard something useful if any of the Shadow's army struck their flock recently. It's a long shot, but Beranabus has devoted his life to long shots.

As we close in on the frantic demons, Kernel stops and stares at a spot close by.

"Come on!" Beranabus shouts. "Don't stop now. We —"

"A window's opening," Kernel says, and Beranabus instantly loses interest in everything else.

"Start opening one of your own," the magician barks, moving ahead of Kernel to protect him from whatever might come through. I step up beside the ancient magician, heart pounding hard for the first time in ages.

"Wait," Kernel says as Beranabus drains magic from the air. "It's not a demon." He studies the invisible lights, then smiles. "We have company."

A few seconds later, a window of dull orange light forms and the Disciple known as Shark emerges, quickly followed by Dervish's old friend, Meera Flame.

"Shark!" Kernel shouts happily.

"Meera!" I yell, even happier than Kernel.

Beranabus glares suspiciously at the pair.

Meera wraps her arms around me and I whirl her off her feet. We're both laughing. She kisses my cheeks. "You've grown," she hoots. "You must be eight feet tall by now!"

"Not quite," I chuckle, setting her down and beaming. Meera used to stay with us a lot and helped me look after Dervish when he was incapacitated a few years back. I had a big crush on Meera when I was younger. Hell, looking at her in her tight leather pants and jacket, I realize I still do. She's a bit on the old side but doesn't show it. If only she had a thing for younger guys!

Kernel and Shark are shaking hands, both talking at the same time. I've never seen Kernel this animated. Shark's wearing army fatigues, looking much the same as ever.

"Hi, Shark," I greet the ex-soldier.

He frowns at me. "Do I know you?"

"Grubbs Grady. We . . ." I stop. I've met Shark twice before, but the first time was in a dream, and the second was in a future that we diverted. As far as he's concerned, I'm a stranger. It's simpler not to explain our previous encounters, especially as I saw him ripped to bits by demons the second time.

"Dervish told me about you," I lie. "I'm Grubbs, his nephew."

Shark nods. "I can see a bit of him in you. But you've got more hair. You're a lot taller too — what's Beranabus been feeding you?"

"Enough of the prattle," Beranabus snaps. "What's wrong?"

As soon as he says that, the mood switches. Shark and Meera's grins disappear.

"We were attacked," Meera says. "I was at Dervish's. We —"

"Was it Lord Loss?" Beranabus barks. "Is Bec all right?"

"She's fine," Shark says.

"But Dervish . . . ," Meera adds, shooting me a worried glance.

My heart freezes. Not Dervish! Losing my parents, Gret, and Bill-E was horrific. Dervish is all I have left. If he's gone too, I don't know if I can continue.

"He was alive when we left," Shark says.

"But in bad shape," Meera sighs. "He had a heart attack."

"We have to go back," I gasp, turning for the window.

Shark puts out a hand to stop me. My eyes flash on the letters S H A R K tattooed across his knuckles, and the picture of a shark's head set between his thumb and index finger.

"Hold on," he says. "We didn't come here directly. That leads to another demon world."

"Besides," Kernel adds, "if the demons are still at the house . . ."

"We weren't attacked by demons," Meera says. "They were . . ." She locks gazes with me and frowns uncertainly. *"Werewolves."*

We gape at her. Then, without discussing it, Kernel turns away and his hands become a blur as he sets about opening a window back to the human universe.

✠ Beranabus crosses first. I'm not far behind. I find myself in a hospital corridor. It looks like the ward where they keep newborn babies. Bec is on the floor close to us. There are two demons. One has the features of an anteater, but sports several snouts. The other is some sort of lizard. Beranabus is addressing them with savage politeness — he's ultra protective of his little Bec.

"What do the pickings look like now?" he asks as Kernel, Shark, and Meera step through after us. In response, the demons bolt for safety. Kernel and the Disciples race after them.

"Dervish?" I snap at Bec, not giving a damn about demons, babies, or anything else except my uncle.

"Back there," Bec pants, pointing back down the corridor. "Hurry. He was fighting a demon. I don't know —"

I run as fast as I can, long strides, readying myself for the worst. I glance into each room that I pass. Signs of struggle and death in some of them, but no Dervish. I pause at the door of what looks to be an empty room. I'm about to push on when something grunts.

Entering, I spot Dervish to my left, half-obscured by an overturned bed. There's a demon on top of him, shaped like a giant insect with a golden shell. It's snapping at Dervish's face, mandibles grinding open and shut. I'm on it in an instant. I make a fist and smash through its protective shell. It shrieks and turns to deal with me, but I fill its guts with fire and it dies screaming. When I'm sure it's dead, I toss it aside and bend over my startled, bleary-eyed uncle. He slaps at me feebly. Doesn't recognize me. He's finding it hard to focus.

"Hey, baldy," I chuckle. "Things must be bad when you can't squish a damn cockroach."

Dervish relaxes and his eyes settle on me. The smile that lights his face is almost enough to bring me to tears.

"Grubbs!" he cries, throwing his arms around me.

"Don't go all blubbery on me," I mutter into his shoulder, fighting back sobs.

Dervish pushes himself away, touches my face with wonder, then says in that wry tone I recall so well, "You could have sent me a card while you were away."

"No post offices," I grunt, and we beam at each other.

✠ Waiting while the Disciples cleanse the hospital of demons. I should help them, but this will probably be the only private time I get with Dervish. Things have a habit of moving swiftly when Beranabus gets involved. Once they finish off the last demon, talk will turn to the werewolf attack and there might not be any time to sit with my uncle and chat. I've devoted a huge chunk of my life to Beranabus's cause. I'm due a few minutes of down time.

"I told you healthy eating wasn't worthwhile," I say, nudging Dervish in the ribs (but gently — he looks like blood mixed in with lumpy porridge). "You told me I should watch my diet. But who had a heart attack first?"

"As illogical as ever." Dervish scowls. "I thought you might have matured while you were away, but obviously you haven't."

"Seriously, how have you been?" I ask.

"Apart from the heart attack?"

"Yeah."

He shrugs, looking older than I'd have thought possible. "I'm about ready to follow Billy into the wide blue yonder."

My face stiffens. "Don't say that, not even joking."

"No joke," he sighs. "I was given a single task by Beranabus — guard the entrance to the cave — and I screwed it up. I told Billy's mom I'd look after him — some job I did of that. I took you in and promised you'd be safe with me, then . . ."

"I *was* safe with you."

"Yeah, I really protected you. Lord Loss and his familiars didn't get anywhere near you on my watch, did they?"

"That wasn't your fault," I tell him heavily. "You did the best you could. For me *and* Bill-E."

"Then why is he dead and why are you lost to me?" Dervish moans.

"Because we live in a world under siege," I say. "Life

sucks for mages and magicians — *you* taught me that. Bad things happen to those of us who get involved, but if we didn't fight, we'd be in an even worse state. None of it's your fault, any more than it's the fault of the moon or the stars."

Dervish nods slowly, then arches an eyebrow. *"The moon or the stars?"*

"I always get poetic when I'm dealing with self-pitying simpletons."

We laugh. This is what I love best about my relationship with Dervish — the more we insult each other, the happier we are. I'm trying to think of something disgusting and hair-curling to say when Beranabus appears. He's using baby wipes to clean his hands.

"Still alive?" he asks Dervish.

"Just about."

"We're finished here. Time to go."

It's not fair. We've only had a few minutes together. I want to ask Dervish about Bec and how they're coping. How he explained Bill-E's disappearance to our neighbors. What's happening with my friends. I want to complain about my life with Beranabus and boast about all the action I've seen.

But those are childish, selfish wishes. We're in the middle of a maternity ward. I've seen several dead and dismembered bodies already — nurses, mothers, babies. There are probably dozens more scattered throughout the hospital. I'd be the shallowest person in the universe if, in the face of all that tragedy, I moaned of not having enough time to spend with my uncle.

"Where are we going?" I ask.

"The roof," Beranabus says. "We need to discuss the situation before moving on. It's more complicated than we thought. Bec says the demons who struck were led by Juni Swan." Dervish and I stare incredulously, then we both start to shout questions at him. "Not now!" Beranabus stops us. "We'll talk about it on the roof."

"I don't think I can make it that far," Dervish says.

Beranabus mutters something under his breath — it sounds like, "I hate the damn Gradys!" — then picks up Dervish.

"I can carry him," I say quickly.

"No," Beranabus grunts. "Keep watch for any demons we might have missed."

Settling Dervish on his back, the magician heads for the stairs. I follow a few feet behind, eyes peeled for monsters all the way up the blood-drenched steps to the roof.

NEW MISSION

✠ ✠ ✠

THE voice of the Kah-Gash whispers to me as we're climbing the stairs, stunning me by abruptly breaking its months-long silence. *You can join with the others.*

I pause, startled by its sudden and unexpected reappearance. Then, not wanting to let Beranabus know — he might toss Dervish aside in his eagerness to make enquiries of the Kah-Gash — I carry on as normal, addressing it internally. "What do you mean?"

Can't you feel the magic inside Bec and Kernel calling to you?

I have been feeling a strange tickling sensation since I stepped through the window. I put it down to chemical irritants in the air — one thing you can't say about the demon universe is that it's polluted. I've become accustomed to fume-free atmospheres. But now that the Kah-Gash has clued me in, I realize the tickling is the force within myself straining to unite with Bec and Kernel.

"What would happen if we joined?" I ask.

Wonders.

"Care to be a bit more specific?"

No, it answers smugly. I'm not sure if the Kah-Gash is a parasite feeding off me, or if it's woven into my flesh, a part of me like my heart or brain. But its voice bears echoes of mine. I've used that smart-alec tone more times than I can remember.

I'm worried about letting my piece of the Kah-Gash link with the other parts again. What would it do if I gave it free reign? Could we trust it?

You are the control mechanism, the voice says, the first time it's ever told me anything about the nature of itself. *With my help, you can unify the pieces and unleash your full power.*

"But could we control it," I press, "and make the weapon do our bidding?"

To an extent, the voice answers cagily.

"What does that mean?" I grumble, but there's no reply. "Hello? Are you still there?"

Unite us, it says impatiently. *Unleash me. Become the Kah-Gash.*

"Without knowing what I'm getting myself into? No bloody way!" I snort.

Coward, the Kah-Gash sneers, then falls silent. I feel the tickling sensation fade. I continue up the stairs, brooding on what the voice said and wondering what would have happened if I'd given in to it.

On the roof. Another Disciple, Sharmila Mukherji, was seriously wounded by Juni. Her legs are missing from the thighs down. Beranabus is working on the stumps, using magic to stop the bleeding and patch her up. She's unconscious. It doesn't look to me like she'll ever recover.

Dervish is resting on a hospital trolley. Meera's sitting beside him. Shark's guarding the door to the roof, to turn back any curious humans. The rest of us are gathered around Bec, listening to her story.

She tells us about Juni Swan, who's somehow come back to life in a cancerous mockery of a body. Bec says Juni is insane, but more powerful than before. Dervish blasted her from the roof, catching her by surprise when he recovered from the coma he'd been in since his heart attack. I want to go after her, to finish her off, but Bec is adept at sensing where people and demons are, and she says Juni has already fled. Revenge will have to wait for another night.

I thought it would be awkward being around Bec, that she'd remind me of Bill-E, that I'd feel resentful. When he died, she took over his corpse, came back to life, then remolded the flesh in her original image. In effect, she stole his body. But there's nothing of my half-brother apart from the occasional word or gesture. I have no trouble thinking of her as a separate person with the same right to exist as any other.

Bec speaks quickly, detailing how werewolves attacked our home in Carcery Vale, backed up by humans with guns. She tells us she can absorb people's memories when she touches them. When grappling with a werewolf, she learned it was a Grady boy who'd been handed to the Lambs to be executed. But the Lambs — executioners set up to dispose of teens with the lycanthropic family curse — didn't kill him. Instead they kept him alive, and found a way to use him and other werewolves as trained killers.

"You're sure the Lambs masterminded the attack in Carcery Vale?" I ask.

"I can't be certain," Bec says. "We didn't see any humans. Sharmila wanted to go after the Lambs once Dervish was safe, but we decided to wait until we'd discussed it with you. The werewolves *might* have been the work of some other group. . . ."

"But they were definitely teenagers who'd been given to the Lambs?" I press. If she's right about this, we have a known enemy to target. If she's wrong, I don't want to waste time chasing an irritating but harmless gang of humans.

"Yes," Bec says. "At least the one I touched was. I don't know about the others."

"They must have been," I mutter. "I've never heard of anyone outside our family being inflicted with the wolfen curse. But why?" I glance at Dervish. "Have you been rubbing Prae Athim up the wrong way?" She's the head honcho of the Lambs. Her and Dervish don't see eye to eye on a number of issues.

"I haven't seen her since she paid us that visit before *Slawter*," Dervish answers, looking bewildered. "I've got to say, I don't have much time for Prae, but this isn't her style. I could understand it if they were after something — you, for instance, to dissect you and try to find a cure for lycanthropy — but there was nothing in this for them. Those who set the werewolves loose wanted us dead. The Lambs don't go in for mindless, wholesale slaughter."

"But if not the Lambs, who?" Kernel asks.

"I think Lord Loss was behind the attacks," Bec says. "Maybe he realized I was part of the Kah-Gash and wanted to eliminate the threat I pose, or perhaps he just wanted to kill Dervish and me for revenge. The attack tonight by Juni Swan makes me surer than ever that he sent the werewolves. It can't be coincidence."

"Juni Swan," Beranabus echoes, with the guilty look that crosses his face whenever talk turns to his ex-assistant. "I'd never have thought poor Nadia could turn into such a hideous creature. I don't know how she survived." He looks at Bec. "Your spirit flourished after death, but you're part of the Kah-Gash. Juni isn't. Lord Loss must have separated her soul from her body some way, just before her death. That's why he took her corpse when he fled. But I don't understand how he did it."

He mulls it over, then curses. "It doesn't matter. We can worry about her later. You're right — Lord Loss sent the werewolves. I cast spells on Carcery Vale to prevent crossings, except for in the secret cellar, where any demon who did cross would be confined. Even if he found a way around those spells, he would have been afraid to risk a direct confrontation. If he opened a window, the air would have been saturated with magic. You and Dervish could have tapped into that. You were powerful in the cave, stronger than Lord Loss in some ways. He probably thought humans and werewolves stood a better chance of killing you. But that doesn't explain why the Lambs agreed to help him. Or, if they weren't Lambs, how they got their hands on the werewolves."

"Maybe he struck a deal with them," Dervish says. "Promised them the cure for lycanthropy if they helped him murder Bec and me."

"Would they agree to such a deal?" Beranabus asks.

"Possibly."

"Prae Athim's daughter turned into a werewolf," I say softly, recalling my previous meeting with the icy-eyed Lambs leader. "She's still alive. A person will go to all manner of crazy lengths when family's involved." I shoot Dervish a wink.

"An intriguing mystery," Beranabus snorts. "But we can't waste any more time on it. We have more important matters to deal with, not least the good health of Dervish and Miss Mukherji — they'll both be dead soon if we don't take them to the demon universe. Open a window, Kernel."

Kernel eagerly sets to work on a window. His eyes have held up so far, but they won't last indefinitely. The problem with building body parts in the demon universe is they don't work on this world. If he stays too long, Kernel will end up blind as a bat again, with a pair of gooey sockets instead of eyes.

"I'm not going," Dervish says.

"You can't stay here," Beranabus replies quickly, angrily.

"I have to. They attacked me . . . my home . . . my friends. I can't let that pass. I have to pursue them. Find out why. Exact revenge."

"Later," Beranabus sniffs.

"No," Dervish growls. "Now." He gets off the gurney and almost collapses. Meera grabs him and holds him up. He smiles at her, then glares at Beranabus. He might be within a whisker of death, but that hasn't affected my uncle's fighting spirit.

"It would help if we knew," Meera says quietly in defense of Dervish. "The attack on Dervish and Bec might have been a trial run. The werewolves could be set loose on other Disciples."

"That's not my problem," Beranabus says callously. He's never been overly bothered about his supporters, and always stresses the fact that they sought him out and chose to follow him — he didn't recruit them.

"There's been a huge increase in crossings," Meera says, which is troubling news to me. "We've seen five or six times the usual activity in recent months. The Disciples are stretched thinly, struggling to cope. If several were picked off by werewolves and assassins, thousands of innocents would die."

"It might be related," Kernel says, pausing and looking back.

"Related to what?" Bec asks, but Beranabus waves her question away. He's frowning, waiting for Kernel to continue.

"This could be part of the Shadow's plan," Kernel elaborates. "It could be trying to create scores of windows so that its army of demons can break through at once. We'll need the Disciples if that's the case — we can't be everywhere at the same time to stop them all."

"Maybe," Beranabus hums. "But that doesn't alter the fact that Dervish will last about five minutes if we leave him here."

"I'll be fine," Dervish snarls.

"No," Beranabus says. "Your heart is finished. You'll die within days. That's not a guess," he adds when Dervish starts to argue. "And you wouldn't be able to do much during that time, apart from wheeze and clutch your chest a lot."

Dervish stares at the magician, badly shaken. I'm appalled too. "It's really that bad?" Dervish croaks.

Beranabus nods, and I can see that he's enjoying bringing Dervish down a peg. He doesn't like people who challenge his authority. "In the universe of magic, you might survive. Here, you're a dead man walking."

"Then get him there quick," I say instantly. "I'll stay."

"Not you too," Beranabus groans. "What did I do to deserve as stubborn and reckless a pair as you?"

"It makes sense," I insist calmly. "If the attacks were Lord Loss trying to get even, they're irrelevant. But if they're related to the Shadow, we need to know. I can confront the Lambs, find out if they're mixed up with the demon master, stop them if they are."

"Is the Shadow the creature we saw in the cave?" Bec asks.

"Aye," Beranabus says. "We haven't learned much about it, except that it's put together an army of demons and is working hard to launch them across to our world." He stares at me, frowning. He doesn't want to admit that I might have a valid point, but I can tell by his scowl that he knows I do.

"You'd operate alone?" he asks skeptically.

"I'd need help." I glance around. Shark's an obvious choice. I can channel a lot of magic here, but there are times when it pays to have a thickly built thug on your side. But I'll need someone sharp too — I don't have the biggest of brainboxes. "Shark and Meera," I say, with what I hope sounds like authority. Shark can't hear me, but to my surprise Meera responds negatively.

"I want to stay with Dervish," she says.

"He'll be fine," I tell her, trying to sound confident, not wanting them to know how nervous I feel — I've never taken on a mission like this before. "He has Beranabus and Bec to look after him. Unless you want to leave Bec with me?" I ask the magician.

"No," he mumbles, as I guessed he would. "If you're staying, I'll take her to replace you."

"Then go," I say. "Chase the truth on your side. I'll do the same here. If I discover no link between Lord Loss and the Lambs, I'll return. If they *are* working for him, I'll cull the whole bloody lot."

Kernel grunts and a green window opens. "Time to decide," he tells Beranabus. I look from the magician to Meera. She's not happy, but she doesn't raise any further objections.

"Very well," Beranabus snaps. "But listen to Shark and Meera, heed their advice and contact me before you go running up against the likes of Lord Loss or the Shadow." He picks up the unconscious Sharmila. "Follow me, Bec," he says curtly and steps through the window.

Bec stares at us, confused. I flash her a quick grin of support, which she misses. Meera steps up to her and asks if she's OK. Before I can hear her reply, Dervish is hugging me, squeezing me tight.

"I don't want to leave you," he says, and I can tell he's struggling not to cry. I have a lump in my throat too.

"You have to go," I tell him. "You'll die if you stay here."

"Maybe that would be the easiest thing," he sighs.

I squeeze his ribs until he gasps. "Don't you dare give up," I snarl. "Mom and Dad . . . Gret and Bill-E . . . they'd give anything to be where you are now alive. It doesn't matter how much pain you're in or how sorry you feel for yourself. Alive is better than dead. Always."

"When did you become the sensible one?" Dervish scowls.

"When you became a pathetic mess," I tell him lightly.

"Oh." He grins. "Thanks for clearing that up." He clasps the back of my neck and glares into my eyes. "Be careful, Grubbs. If you die before me, I'll be mad as hell."

"Don't worry," I laugh. "I'll outlive you by decades. I'll be dancing on your grave fifty years from now, just wait and see."

Dervish smiles shakily, then releases me and staggers through the window, massaging his chest with one hand, just about managing not to weep. I hate watching him go. I wish he could stay or that I could leave with him. But wishes don't mean a damn when you've been selected by the universe to spend your life fighting demons.

"Sorry we couldn't have more of a chat," I say to Bec, and I genuinely mean it. I'd like to sit down with her and listen to her full story, learn what life was like sixteen hundred years ago, what she makes of the world now, if *Riverdance* is anything like the real deal.

"Next time." She smiles.

"Yeah," I grunt, not believing for a second that our paths will cross again. In this game you soon learn not to take anything good for granted. The chances are that Bec or I — probably both — will perish at the hands of demons long before the universes can throw us back together.

I think about bidding Kernel farewell, but he doesn't look interested in saying goodbye, so I simply wave at him. He half-waves back, already focusing on Bec. She's his companion now. I mean nothing to him if I'm not by his side, so he won't waste time worrying about me. I know how he feels because I feel the same way about him.

"Come on," I say to a slightly befuddled-looking Meera. "Let's go and break the news to Shark. Do you think he'll mind us volunteering him for a life-or-death mission?"

"No," Meera sighs as we cross the roof to the doorway. "That dumb goon would be offended if we left him out."

GETTING STARTED

✠ ✠ ✠

IT'S chaos downstairs. Juni Swan forced down a helicopter during the duel on the roof. The flames are still flickering, though the teams of firefighters who were quick on the scene have the worst of the blaze under control. Shattered glass from the hospital windows lines the surrounding streets like crystal confetti. The dead and wounded are everywhere, covered in blankets or being nursed by bloodied, shaken medics. Police buzz around like angry bees.

Shark has no problem talking his way through. A few words with the commanding officer and we're being escorted past the teams of baying news reporters to a spot in the city where we're free to go our own way. The Disciples have contacts in some pretty high places.

First things first — we're exhausted and need to sleep. We find the nearest hotel and book three connecting rooms. The receptionist regards us warily and almost refuses us entry, but when Shark produces a platinum credit card and says he'll pay up front, and that he wants their best rooms, the man behind the desk undergoes a swift transformation.

I'd like to talk through events with Shark and Meera, but both disappear to their beds as soon as we've tipped the bellboy and shut the doors, so I've no choice but to follow their lead.

The room's large, but it feels cramped after a year spent sleeping wild — if not often — beneath vast demonic skies. I open the windows and stick my head out, breathing in fresh air as I replay the scenes from the hospital. Why the hell did I volunteer to stay behind? I could be with Dervish now, catching up, taking care of him. Instead I've promised to track down Prae Athim and put a stop to whatever's going on between Lord Loss and the Lambs. Just *how* I'm going to do that is a mystery. I spoke before I thought, like an overeager hero. I've been hanging around Beranabus too long!

Withdrawing, I decide the plans can wait. I go to the bathroom, then undress and slide beneath the soft bedcovers. I'm worried I won't be able to sleep, that I'll lie awake all night. But within a minute my eyelids go heavy, and seconds later it's lights out.

✠ Breakfast in bed is heavenly. I eat like a ravenous savage, bolting down sausages, bacon, eggs, mushrooms. And toast! How can a few burnt bits of bread smeared with churned-up cow's milk taste so delicious?

There's a knock on one of the connecting doors while I'm mopping up the juice from my baked beans. "C'm' in," I grunt.

Meera appears like an angel, in an ivory-white nightdress. Washed, manicured, the works. You'd never guess that twelve hours earlier she'd been elbow-deep in demon blood.

"Wow!" I exclaim, dropping the toast and clapping.

She beams and gives me a twirl, then perches on the edge of my bed and picks up the toast. "Do you mind?"

"Not at all." I grin, though I'd have bitten the hand off anybody else who tried to take my last piece.

"I've been up for hours," she says.

"You should have woken me."

"Why? Did you want a manicure too?"

"Very funny. But I could have done with a haircut."

"That's for sure," she sniffs. "I ordered some clothes for you. I can't wait to see you in them. I love dressing up boys, especially fashion-challenged teens."

"Me? Fashion-challenged? I never used to be."

"Well, you are now." She takes my tray and tugs at the bedsheets. "Come on. Chop-chop!"

"Whoah!" I yelp, only just managing to grab on to the sheets in time. "I'm naked under here!"

"That's OK," she says. "You sleepwalked into my room last night and did a dance on my rug. I saw it all then."

I stare at her, more horrified than I've been in the face of any demon. Then she winks wickedly and races out of the room before I batter her to death with a pillow.

Shark's the last to rise. We hold a conference in his room while he tucks into lunch, wearing a robe that just about covers his privates.

“So,” he mumbles through a half full mouth. “What’s the plan?”

I scratch my head and smile sheepishly. “I kind of hoped you guys would have one. . . .”

Shark and Meera share a wry glance.

“I thought you were our leader,” Meera says.

“You set the ball rolling,” Shark agrees. “We just came along for the ride.”

“I don’t know what to do,” I grumble. “It was easy in the demon universe. We cornered demons, beat them up, and sometimes killed them. It’s different here. I don’t know where to start. How will we find Prae Athim? It seemed like the simplest thing in the world last night, but now . . .”

“Not such a big shot in the cold light of day, is he?” Shark jeers.

“Don’t tease him,” Meera tuts. “It was brave of him to volunteer.”

“But stupid.” Shark points a thick finger at me. “What use are you to us? Why shouldn’t we leave you here and pick you up when it’s all over?”

Stung, I focus on the bed. The mattress quivers and comes alive. It throws off the startled Shark, then bucks from the bed and lands on his back, driving him down. He lashes out, bellowing with alarm, but the mattress smashes him flat and pounds at him relentlessly.

“Enough,” Meera says softly, laying a hand on my shoulder.

I scowl at her, then ease up. I’m sweating slightly.

A bruised Shark gets to his feet, smoothes his robe, and studies me calmly. “OK, I’m impressed. You’re a magician?”

"Yes."

"How powerful are you?"

I shrug. "I never really tested myself on this world. That trick with the mattress tired me, but I could do a lot more."

"How much more?" Shark presses.

"No idea," I answer honestly. "But in the absence of any windows between universes, I'm stronger than any mage we'll face."

"I suppose we might as well bring him along," Shark says grudgingly to Meera.

"Where do we start?" Meera asks. "Do you know where Prae Athim's based?"

"I never even heard of her before last night," Shark says. "I knew about the Grady werewolves and the Lambs, but they were never my problem. Still, this won't be the first time I've gone looking for someone. We'll find her."

"We could do with some help," Meera notes. "They have armed troops, as we saw in Carcery Vale."

"The Disciples?" Shark asks.

"The Disciples," Meera agrees.

The pair produce cell phones and start dialing.

The mages aren't interested in our mission. This is a bad time for humanity. Demons are attempting to cross faster, and in greater numbers, than ever before. The Disciples are rushed off their feet, dashing from one crisis to another. There have been six successful crossings this year and more than a dozen foiled attempts. And those are only the recorded attacks — more probably went unnoticed. Over five hundred people that we know of have died, not including those at the hospital last night. That's an average decade's worth of action.

The Disciples that Shark and Meera chat with over the course of the day don't care about werewolves or the Lambs. They don't even respond when told that Beranabus is involved. Most times, the mere mention of his name is enough to whip them into action. But not now. We can fight our own battles as far as they're concerned.

Shark and Meera turn to their other allies when the Disciples fall through. They have a network of contacts — soldiers, politicians, police officers, doctors, etc. They call on them for support when demons cross and create merry hell. The operatives move in to clear up the mess, bury the dead, comfort the survivors, kill the story before it spreads.

Meera's contacts are mostly media types and corporate directors. She calls around, asking about the Lambs, but the Grady executioners keep a low profile. She learns that they have several worldwide bases, but Prae Athim could be at any of them.

Shark takes a different approach. He phones a guy called Timas Brauss and tells him to come as swiftly as possible. He then contacts people in armies or who were once soldiers. He sets about assembling a small unit of men and women with a variety of skills — explosives experts, mechanics, pilots, scuba divers, and more. He won't need them all, but he puts in place a large force to draw from. They're more cooperative than the Disciples. Shark seems to command a lot of respect in military circles.

The calls continue into the night. It's the most frustrating day I've spent in a long time. There's nothing I can do except sit, listen, and run errands for Shark or Meera, fetching them food and drink.

I try to watch TV, but I can't get comfortable. I'm worried that Shark and Meera will think I'm slacking. Eventually I crawl into bed, tired and grumpy, thinking I should have stayed in the demon universe. At least I served some bloody good over there!

THE FILTHY TWELVE

✠ ✠ ✠

MY phone rings unexpectedly. Jolted awake, I check the time on the bedside clock — 7:49 AM. Picking up the phone, I yawn, "Yes?"

"It's me," someone says in a strange accent.

"Who?"

A pause. "You're not Shark."

"No, I'm Grubbs. Shark's in the next room. Do you want me to —"

"It doesn't matter," he interrupts. "I'm Timas Brauss. Tell the receptionist to let me up."

A couple of minutes later there's a knock on my door. I open it to find an incredibly tall, thin man in the corridor. He must be three inches taller than me. Skinny as a stick insect, with long, bony fingers. Floppy red hair, an even darker shade than mine. A startled pair of blue eyes, as if he's in a constant state of shock.

He pushes past me without a word. Looks around the

room and up at the ceiling. He's carrying a couple of laptops and a briefcase. He sets them down, then drags the desk by the wall out into the middle of the floor and lays his gear on top of it. Fires up the laptops, takes a few plug-ins out of the briefcase, and connects them up.

"Wi-Fi is a blessing from the gods," he mutters as I stare at him. "It was hell on Earth when I had to hook these up to ordinary phone lines. Who are we looking for?"

"A woman called . . ." I hesitate. "Do you want me to wake Shark?"

Timas shakes his head. "I can work without him. Who are you after?"

"Prae Athim."

"Spell it."

When I've done that, I tell him she works for an organization called the Lambs. I start to describe the attacks and why we want to find her, but he holds up a hand. "That is enough information for me to be getting on with," he says curtly, and bends over his laptops like a pianist. He's soon tapping away at a fierce speed, oblivious to all else, working on both computers at the same time.

Meera wakes before Shark. She's surprised to find the odd-looking stranger in my room, but says nothing once I've told her in whispers of his approach to business. We eat breakfast, then return to watch Timas Brauss. At one stage I ask if he'd like anything to eat or drink. He shushes me without looking up.

Shark finally rises close to midday. When he steps in to find Timas hard at work, he doesn't look surprised. Stretching, he nods at Meera and me, then grunts at the man hunched over the laptops. "What do you have?"

Timas spins neatly to face Shark, letting his fingers rest on his knees. He looks like an overgrown schoolboy. "I have a full profile of the woman, Prae Argietta Athim. Do you want to know her background?"

"Couldn't care less," Shark sniffs. "Where is she?"

Timas clicks his tongue. "I would need more time to answer definitively. But I can tell you where she should be if she's adhering to her regular schedule."

"That'll do," Shark says.

Timas reads out a long address, down to the zip code, finishing off with her floor and office number.

"It's a regular building?" Shark asks.

"Yes. The Lambs own the complex. A mix of offices, laboratories, and miscellaneous divisions. I've downloaded a schematic plan of the structure and environs."

"Let's see." Shark pushes Timas aside and studies the right-hand screen. Meera and I edge over to look at it with him. The blueprints mean nothing to me — my eyes go blurry from looking at all the lines — but Shark nods happily as he scrolls down. "Should be easy enough to crack. Security systems?"

"Downloading," Timas says, tapping the other laptop.

"How much longer?"

"Maybe an hour. They are very cleverly protected. An invigorating challenge."

Shark stretches again. He looks pleased. "Unless they've packed the corridors with troops, this should be a piece of cake. We'll put a small team together, waltz in, grab Prae Athim, shake her up . . . be home in time for supper."

"You really think it'll be that easy?" Meera asks skeptically.

"Like hell." Shark grins. "But you know me — ever the optimist."

While Timas continues to play his keyboards, Shark gets back on the phone with those on his shortlist. Meera also makes a few calls, in case any of her contacts have discovered anything about the Lambs. I sit around as impatiently as the day before, twiddling my thumbs.

The first of Shark's team arrives at five, a chunky woman called Pip LeMat, an explosives expert. She's followed by three men over the course of the evening — James Farrior, Leo DeSalle, and Spenser Holm. They're all soldiers but I don't learn much more about them. They retire with Pip and Shark to his room shortly after they arrive, making it clear they don't want to be disturbed. Apart from the clinking of bottles and glasses, and the occasional cheer or bellow, we don't hear from them for the rest of the night.

Shortly before eleven, Timas steps away from his laptops, takes a blue satin handkerchief from a pocket and dabs at his forehead, then folds it neatly and puts it away again. "Could I have some milk and a selection of whatever pastries the hotel has in stock?" he asks.

"Pastries?" Meera frowns. "This late?"

"Yes, please," Timas says calmly. "I would like an ice pack also, for my frontal cranium, and could you please make up a cot for me beside the desk?"

"I'm sure we can find a room for you," Meera says.

"No thank you," Timas replies. "I would prefer a cot."

"I'll see what I can rustle up," Meera says, then whispers to me, "I'm going back to my room when I'm finished. This guy gives me the creeps."

I hide a smile, wait until she's gone, then ask Timas how he knows Shark.

"He killed my father," Timas says in a neutral tone, studying the back of the TV and frowning with disapproval.

Timas's English is excellent, but it's clearly not his first language. I think he must have made a mistake. "Do you mean he worked with your father?" I ask.

"No. He killed him. My father was trying to summon a demon. He meant to sacrifice me and my sister as part of the ritual. Shark saved me."

"And your sister?"

"He was not in time to help her." Timas walks around the rest of the room, making a survey of the remote controls, light fixtures, telephones . . . everything electronic.

"Shark felt he was to blame for my sister's death," Timas says. "He should have saved her. He didn't react quickly enough. Guilt-ridden, he developed an interest in my future. I was already heavily involved with computers, so he put me in touch with people who knew more than I did. I worked with them for a time, then with some others. When Shark realized I was the best in my field and could be of use to him, he re-established contact.

"I relished the challenge I was given and indicated my desire to work with him on subsequent projects. He summons me every so often. I drop everything to assist him. The people I work for understand. They know how important Shark's work is. Do you work for Shark too?"

"Not exactly. We're . . . associates." The word doesn't sound right, but I don't want Timas thinking I'm Shark's lackey.

Timas thinks about that for a moment, then sighs. "I hope they have *pain au chocolat.* That's my favorite." Then he falls silent and stares at his laptops, not moving a muscle, barely even blinking.

Four more soldiers arrive the next morning, three men and one woman. Shark introduces them only by their first names — Terry, Liam, Stephen, and Marian. They don't show any interest in Meera or me, so we don't bother with them either. Probably better that way. If we have to fight, some of us might die, and it's easier to cope with the death of someone you're not friendly with.

"Has it clicked yet?" Shark asks as we gather in my room around Timas, who's beavering away at his laptops after a short night's sleep.

"Huh?" I frown.

"Do a head count. Twelve of us. *The Dirty Dozen.* I love that film."

"I hope that's not your only reason for deciding on that number," I growl.

"It's as good a reason as any," he chuckles. "But that wasn't the key factor. I have access to a helicopter and it holds twelve. I could have commissioned a larger craft but I'm familiar with this model. I can fly it if I have to, though James will be doing most of the flying — he's the best pilot I know. Handy with a rifle too. If we need a sniper, James Farrier's our man."

"What's Timas like with a gun?" I ask.

"Not bad," Shark says. "But it needs to be a high-tech weapon with some kind of computer chip. He doesn't like ordinary guns, but if you hand him something complicated that he can play with, he's in his element."

"Timas isn't altogether there, is he?" I mutter.

Shark smiles. "You think he's a loon. Most people do. But he's passed every test he's ever been given. He's been probed by experts and they've all come away saying he's weird, but nothing more. In theory, he's as sane as you and me."

Shark moves into the middle of the room, takes up position beside Timas, and claps loudly. We cluster around him in a semicircle. Timas looks up, but keeps an eye on his laptops.

"No long speeches," Shark says. "You know I don't call for help unless things are bad. We need to find a woman. She might be mixed up with some seriously dangerous demons. If not, it'll be a walk in the park.

"But if we've guessed right, it'll get nasty. We're talking direct contact with powerful members of the Demonata. We don't want to fight. We only want to establish a link between the woman and the demons. But things could swing out of control and we might find ourselves in over our heads. If we do, you're all dead. You should know that now, before we begin, so you have the chance to back out."

Shark waits. Nobody says anything.

"Figured as much," he barks. "Timas — you got everything we need?" Timas removes USB sticks from both laptops, slips them into his shirt pocket, and nods. "Then let's go," Shark says, and the hunt begins.

MEERA'S WAY

✠ ✠ ✠

WE take a commercial flight. One of Shark's contacts meets us at the airport before we fly out, with tickets and fake passports for those who need them. The photo of me is a few years old. I don't recognize it.

"Where'd you get this?" I ask.

"I found it on the Web," Timas answers. "You were photographed when committed to an institute for the mentally unbalanced. After your parents were killed?" he adds, as if I might have forgotten.

"No wonder I look like a zombie," I mutter, running my thumb over the face in the passport, remembering those dark days of madness. I used to think life couldn't possibly get any worse. How little I knew.

We sit in pairs on the plane, splitting up so as not to attract attention. I'm with Timas. I'd rather have sat with Meera, but James moved quickly to snag the seat next to her. He's chatting her up. I try keeping an eye on them, but as soon as the engines start, my stomach clenches and I grip the armrests tight, flashing back on my most recent experience in a plane.

"Do you want to know the statistics for global aeronautical accidents for the last decade?" Timas asks as we taxi out to the runway.

"No," I growl.

"I only ask because you look uneasy. Many airplanes crash every year, but they are usually personal craft. Statistically we are safer in the air than on the ground. I thought familiarity with the facts might help."

"The last time I was on a plane, demons attacked, slaughtered everyone aboard, and forced it down," I snarl.

"Oh." Timas looks thoughtful. "To the best of my knowledge, there are no statistics on demon-related accidents in the air. I must investigate this further when time permits. There are blanks to be filled in."

He leans back and stares up at the reading light, lips pursed. After a minute he switches the light on, then off again. On. Off. On. Off. The engines roar. We hurtle down the runway and up into the sky. Timas's eyes close after a while and he snores softly. But his finger continues to operate the light switch, turning it on and off every five seconds, irritating the hell out of me.

Another of Shark's crew is waiting for us when we touch down. We drive in a van to a nearby hangar and park outside, close to a large silver helicopter. Shark's soldiers are laughing and joking with each other, excited by the prospect of adventure. They tumble out of the van and circle the helicopter. James pats it and purrs. "This is my baby now. The Farrier Harrier. Bring it on!"

"Statistically, helicopters are not as reliable as airplanes," Timas remarks, but I pretend I didn't hear that.

We take our seats. James invites Meera to sit up front with him, but to my delight she sniffs airily and gives him the cold shoulder.

"You can sit beside me," I tell her, and with a warm smile she accepts my offer. James glares at me and I smirk back.

Timas takes the seat beside James. He's fascinated by the banks of control panels. He asks a couple of questions, then observes silently as James fires up the propellors. I can see Timas's reflection in the glass. He switches between frowns and smiles as he watches the pilot at work.

"I've saved the best for last," Shark roars as we rise smoothly. There are headsets with microphones but nobody's bothered to put them on. Shark stands, bending to avoid hitting his head on the ceiling, and jerks his seat up to reveal a hidden compartment crammed with guns.

The cabin fills with excited "Ooohs!" and "Aaahs!", audible even over the noise of the blades. Shark passes the weapons around to the eager soldiers. I shake my head when he offers me one. I've no experience with guns and I don't want to learn. Magic's cleaner and more effective. Meera doesn't bother with a gun either.

"What about rifles?" Pip shouts, having loaded her gun and jammed it into her waistband.

"And grenades?" Stephen yells.

"Stacks of them." Shark grins. "We'll break them out during the journey. It'll help pass the time."

Meera and I roll our eyes at each other and turn our attention to the scenery beneath. We watch the ground roll away behind us, airport hangars giving way to open countryside dotted with farms and the occasional house. After a while the houses multiply, becoming small villages and towns, feeding into the suburbs of the city where we're headed for our showdown with Prae Athim and her werewolf-armed Lambs.

With Timas navigating, we soon locate the building. It looks like any other, lots of glass and steel, nothing special. Luckily it has a flat roof, and although it's not intended for helicopter landings, Timas assures us that it's structurally sound and will support our weight.

"Headsets!" Shark bellows. When we're all hooked up, he outlines the plan. "James stays with the helicopter — he'll hover nearby after dropping us off. Once we're on the roof, we'll force our way down the staircase to the eleventh floor. Terry and Spenser will stay on the staircase to keep it clear. Leo will take out the elevator. There's another staircase — Marian and Liam will head for that. The rest of us will hit Prae Athim's office."

"What if she's not there?" Meera asks.

"Then we'll find out where she is."

"Don't you think that's a rather heavy-handed approach?" Meera challenges him. "If she's elsewhere and gets wind of our attack, we'll lose the element of surprise."

"You have another idea?"

"Yes," Meera says calmly. "We ask them to let us in."

Shark laughs, then scowls. "You're serious?"

"Absolutely. Politeness often succeeds where brute force fails."

"Brute force has always worked pretty well for me," Shark disagrees.

Meera flashes him her sweetest smile. "Let's try it my way. If it doesn't work, we can hit them hard, but at least we have options. If we do it your way, there's no plan B."

"It's always good to have a plan B," Terry chips in.

"It can't hurt to try her approach," James says from the front of the helicopter. I'm sure he's only saying it to score points with Meera.

"OK." Shark shrugs. "Take us in, Farrier. Meera, it's your show — for now."

As Meera talks us through her simple plan, we drift in over the building, hover closer to the roof, then set down. James kills the blades and as silence settles over us, we sit in place and wait.

Security guards soon spill onto the roof. Thirty or more. They're all armed, but only with handguns.

"A few are ex-military," Leo murmurs, studying the guards as they fan out. "But most look to have been privately trained. We could take them with our eyes shut."

"Leave the *taking* for a while," Meera says, and slides out of the helicopter. She nods for Shark and me to accompany her. As Shark moves forward, she tuts and looks pointedly at his weapons — a couple of revolvers and a small rifle strung across his back.

"Do I have to?" Shark pouts. Meera raises an eyebrow. Sighing, he drops his weapons and clambers out in a foul mood.

We take several steps away from the helicopter, then wait, hands in plain sight. One of the guards — an officer — speaks into a microphone attached to his shirt, waits for orders, then comes to meet us. His troops train their guns on us but keep them slightly lowered, so if one of them fires by accident he won't draw blood.

The officer stops a few feet in front of us. He's wearing a ring with a large gold L set in the center. Prae Athim wore a similar ring when I met her.

"Can I help you folks?" the officer asks with forced politeness.

"We have an appointment," Meera replies smoothly.

The officer seemed prepared for any answer except that one. He blinks stupidly. "An appointment," he echoes.

"With Prae Athim. Could you tell her Meera Flame and Co are here?"

"We're not expecting any visitors," the guard says, his voice taking on a slightly threatening tone.

"*You* might not be" — Meera smiles — "but Prae is. Let her know we're here and I'm sure she'll authorize our entry."

The guard looks troubled. He tells us to stay where we are. Moving out of earshot, he speaks into his microphone again. After a short conversation he calls to us. "Somebody's coming up. Please maintain your positions."

The guard returns to the ranks and waits with the others. As he passes orders along, the guards lower their weapons another fraction. I start to relax. Looks like they don't mean to turn this into a shooting match. At least not yet.

A couple of minutes later, as Shark fidgets, the door to the roof opens and a tall, handsome, tanned man emerges. He's wearing a suit, but no tie. His hair looks like a film star's, thick and carefully waxed into shape. He smiles smoothly and his teeth are a perfect pearly white. Meera's right hand shoots to her hair and she tries to pat it into place, suddenly irritated by the sharp wind whipping over the rooftop, making her job impossible.

"Good afternoon," the man says, stopping closer to us than the guard did. He has a smooth voice. "My name's Antoine Horwitzer. How may I be of service?"

"We're looking for Prae Athim," Shark says as Meera gazes open-mouthed at the man. He nudges her in the ribs and she recovers swiftly.

"Yes," she snaps, a red flush of embarrassment spreading from the center of her cheeks. "We have an appointment. Is she here?"

"One would expect her to be present if one had an appointment and had flown in by helicopter to keep it," Antoine chuckles. "But I don't believe you really arranged a meeting, did you, Miss . . . ?"

"Flame," Meera says with a nervous laugh. "Meera Flame."

"She already gave her name to the guard," Shark growls, eyes narrowing.

"Indeed," Antoine says with a little nod. "I was being disingenuous. I wanted to see if she would give the same name again."

"Why shouldn't she? It's her real name."

"And you are . . . ?" Antoine asks.

"Shark."

"No surname?"

"No."

Antoine's smile flickers. Shark can be intense. He's staring at the man in the suit as if pondering whether or not to cut his heart out and eat it.

"If Prae's here, she'll vouch for us," Meera says. "You're correct — we don't have a scheduled meeting. But she'll want to see us."

"What about the rest of your group?" Antoine asks, smile back in place. He waves at the soldiers in the Farrier Harrier. "I'm no expert, but those guns don't look like toys. Will Miss Athim welcome armed thugs as well?"

"They're our traveling companions," Meera says. "They mean no harm."

"What if I asked them to dispose of their weapons and leave the helicopter?"

"No," Shark barks before Meera can answer.

Antoine's brow furrows, giving the impression that he's thinking this over, but I believe he knew exactly what he was going to say before he set foot on the roof. He doesn't look like a man who leaves much to chance.

"I can't admit you unless I know why you've come," Antoine says eventually.

"We can discuss that with Prae if you tell her we're here," Meera replies.

"You're fishing," Antoine chuckles. "You want me to reveal whether or not she's in the building. But I'm not prepared to tell you unless you answer my questions first."

"It's not your place to make a call like that," Meera says icily. "Prae Athim is the CEO. I don't know what your position is, but if you —"

"Actually, there's been a recent managerial shift," Antoine interrupts. "I am the current chief executive. If you wish to proceed, you'll have to deal with me. Otherwise . . ." He shrugs.

"You've replaced Prae Athim?" Meera asks, startled.

"Not in so many words," Antoine answers evasively.

Meera shares a glance with Shark. He's frowning uncertainly. She doesn't look sure of herself either. I decide it's time for me to step in. I've been standing idly on the sidelines long enough.

"We're here to talk about werewolves," I mutter, drawing my shoulders back to create as much of an impression as I can.

Antoine blinks, his smile crumbling. "And you are . . . ?"

"Grubbs," I tell him, then correct myself. "Grubitsch Grady."

"Ah. I've heard of you. Dervish Grady is your uncle."

"Yes."

Antoine doesn't scratch his head — I doubt he'd ever resort to such a common gesture — but his fingers twitch and I think that's what he'd like to do.

"Werewolves attacked Dervish," I say softly. "At his home. In a team. Backed by people with guns." I stare pointedly at the guards.

"This is an interesting development," Antoine says after a short pause. He looks down at his highly polished shoes and this time I get the impression he really is thinking about what to say next.

When he looks up, his eyes are clear. "I think I'd better invite you down to my office. Will you accompany me, please?" He stands to one side and extends a hand towards the door.

"What about the others?" Shark asks, jerking his head at those in the helicopter.

"They're not necessary."

"I want them there," Shark growls. "Weapons and all."

Antoine prods at his lower lip with his tongue. Then, with a shrug, he says, "Why not? I'd hate to be mistaken for a discourteous host."

Shark's surprised. This means we either have nothing to fear, or else Antoine Horwitzer has another team within the building and is confident they can handle ten armed and experienced soldiers.

I think Shark would like to pull out, but we've nowhere else to turn. If we flee now, our investigation will be blown before it's properly begun. Grumbling to himself, he summons the others, leaving only James inside the Harrier.

“He’s going to start the engine,” Shark tells Antoine.

“To be ready for a quick getaway,” Antoine murmurs wryly. “I’d do the same thing in your position.” He winks at me and I find myself smiling. I distrust this man — he’s too smooth — but at the same time I like him.

“Shall we?” Antoine asks as the members of Shark’s team eye up the guards, who look a lot more nervous now that they have a good view of Shark’s Dirty Dozen.

“I’d like you to answer one of our questions first,” Meera says. “Is Prae Athim here or not?”

“Not.” Antoine lets his smile fade. “Miss Athim has been missing for some time. And our core specimens — what Master Grady referred to as werewolves — have vanished too.”

On that baffling, disturbing note, he leads the way into the building. They might be called Lambs, but as we pass out of the sunlight and into the gloom of the staircase, I think of them more as Lions — and we’re entering their den.

ALL THE KING'S WOLVES

✠ ✠ ✠

WE walk down a flight of steps, then squeeze into an elevator, just us and Antoine Horwitzer. If he's nervous about sealing himself in with nine soldiers, he doesn't show it. Presses the button for the eleventh floor and smiles pleasantly as we descend.

No one speaks until the doors open. As Pip and Terry nudge out, Antoine says, "A moment, please." He's tapping the control panel of the elevator. "Could you tell me some more about the attack you mentioned?"

"I thought we were going to do that in your office," Shark growls suspiciously.

"That was my intention," Antoine replies. "But upon reconsideration I think there might be a better place for our discussion. There's no need to go into the full story here, but if you could provide me with just a few details . . ."

Shark looks at Meera. She shrugs, then quickly runs through the attack at Carcery Vale. Antoine listens silently.

His smile never slips, but it starts to strain at the edges. When Meera finishes, he nods soberly and presses a button low on the panel. There's a buzzing noise. Everyone tenses.

"Nothing to worry about," Antoine says calmly, pushing a series of buttons. "I'm taking us to the lower levels. That requires a security code."

"How low does this thing go?" Shark asks.

"There are ten floors beneath the ground," Antoine says. "I thought we'd check out the lower fourth and fifth." He pauses, his finger hovering over the number 2. "This is the final digit. Once I press this, the doors will shut and we'll drop. If you have any objections, this is the time to raise them."

Shark thinks about it, then sniffs as if he hasn't a care in the world. Antoine presses the button. The buzzer stops. The doors slide shut. We slip further into the bowels of the building.

We step out of the elevator and find ourselves in a corridor much like any other. But when we follow Antoine through an ordinary-looking door, we discover something completely unexpected.

We're in a huge, open room, dotted with cages, banks of machines, and steel cabinets. The cages all seem to be several yards square and three or four yards high. Some show evidence of having been inhabited recently — feces and scraps of food litter the floors — but most look like they've never been used.

"This is a holding area," Antoine says, taking us on a tour. "As you can see, we try not to cram too many specimens into one place. Despite this limit, if you'd come here a couple of months ago, you'd have had to wear ear plugs — the din they create is unbelievable."

Timas stops by one of the machines and studies it with interest.

"That locks and unlocks the cage doors," Antoine explains. "There are other devices linked to it — overhead cameras, lights, air conditioner, water hoses, implant initiators."

"Implants?" I ask.

"Most of the specimens are implanted with control chips. In the event of a mass escape, we could disable them within seconds. We take as few risks as possible when dealing with creatures as swift, powerful, and savage as these."

"You don't need such bulky equipment," Timas says disapprovingly.

"It's psychological," Antoine counters. "Staff feel safer if they have a big, obvious machine to turn to in case of an emergency."

"Ah." Timas smiles. "The human factor. What silly beings we are."

Antoine looks at Timas oddly, then leads us out of the room, into a smaller laboratory. There are several people at work, some in white coats, others in normal clothes. Glass cases line the walls. I go cold when I see what's in them — hands, heads, feet, ears, bits of flesh and bone, all taken from deformed humans . . . from *werewolves.*

"What is this?" I croak.

"Unsettling, aren't they?" Antoine remarks, studying a pair of oversized eyes floating in a jar of clear liquid. "I'm not convinced it's necessary for them to be displayed in so lurid a fashion, but our technical geniuses insist —"

"What the hell *is* this?" I shout, losing my temper.

Antoine blinks at me, surprised by my anger. Then his expression clears. "How thoughtless of me. These remains come from relatives of yours. I must apologize for my insensitivity. I never meant to cause offense."

"Don't worry about that," Shark says, squeezing my shoulder to calm me. "But Grubbs is right — what is this place? It looks like Frankenstein's lab."

"To an extent it is." Antoine sighs. "This is where we experiment upon many of our unfortunate specimens. As you know, we've been trying to find the genetic source of the Grady disease for decades, searching for a cure. Our experts need a place to dissect and reassemble, to study and collate. It's an unpleasant business, but no worse, I assure you, than any institute devoted to animal experiments."

"These aren't animals," I snarl. "They're human."

"They were once," Antoine corrects me. "Now . . ." He makes a face. "As you said, your uncle was attacked by werewolves. You didn't qualify that because you don't think of them as humans with a defect. When the genes mutate, the specimens become something inhuman — although, if we ever crack the rogue genes, perhaps we can restore their humanity."

Timas has wandered over to a computer console. "I assume all of your results and data are backed up here."

"They're stored on a mainframe," Antoine says, "but they're accessible through most of the computers in the building if you have clearance."

"You still use mainframes?" Timas tuts. "How primitive." He runs a finger over the keys. "I'd like to study your records. I know nothing of lycanthropy. I find myself intrigued."

"Sorry," Antoine says stiffly. "Our database is off-limits to all but the most strictly authorized personnel. As I'm sure you'll agree, this is a sensitive matter. We wouldn't want just anybody to have access to such incendiary material."

"This is all very interesting," Meera butts in, "but it doesn't explain about Prae Athim or what you said on the roof regarding the missing *specimens*."

"I'm coming to that," Antoine says patiently. "Trust me, this will be simpler if we proceed step by step." He walks ahead of us and turns, gesturing around the room. "As I was saying, we've been extremely busy, cutting specimens up, running tests on live subjects, introducing various chemical substances into the veins of random guinea pigs in the hopes of stumbling upon a cure."

"Any luck?" Shark asks.

"No," Antoine says. "We've plowed untold millions into this project — and others around the globe — with zero success. If not for the continued support of wealthy Gradys, and our dabbling in parallel medical fields, we would have faced bankruptcy long ago."

"'Parallel medical fields'?" Meera echoes.

"We might not have unraveled the mysteries of the Grady genes, but our research has led to breakthroughs in other areas. As a result, we have become a worldwide pharmaceutical giant. Steroids are our speciality, though we're by no means limited to so finite a field."

Antoine looks like he's about to give us a breakdown of the Lambs' success stories. But then, remembering why we're here, he returns to the relevant facts.

"As you can imagine, specimens are difficult to come by. Very few parents wish to hand their children over for medical experimentation, even if they're no longer recognizably human. Many children have been placed in the care of the Lambs in the past, but only to be . . . decommissioned."

"You mean executed," I growl.

Antoine nods slowly. "In most circumstances, the parents never inquire after the child once we take it into custody. The less they know about the grisly details, the better. A few ask for ashes to be returned, but almost nobody requests a body for burial. And since ashes are easy to fake . . ."

"You don't kill them!" I'm furious. This could have happened to Gret or Bill-E. The thought of them winding up here, caged, experimented on, humiliated, treated like lab rats . . . It makes me want to hit somebody. My hands clench into fists and I glare at Antoine. It takes all my self-control not to attack.

"It sounds inhumane," Antoine says quietly. "I admit it's a betrayal of trust. But it's necessary. We do this for the good of the family. I've seen the grief and anguish in the eyes of parents who've watched their children turn into nightmarish beasts. If we have to lie to prevent that from happening to others, so be it."

"It's wrong," I disagree. "They wouldn't have given their children to you if they knew what you planned to do with them."

"True," Antoine says. "But we can't search for a cure without specimens to work on. Isn't it better to experiment than execute? To seek a remedy rather than accept defeat?"

"Not without permission," I mutter obstinately.

"I wish you could see it our way," Antoine sighs. "But I understand your point of view. This is a delicate matter." He looks decidedly miserable now. "But if you can't find any positives in what I've shown you so far, please be warned — you're absolutely going to hate what I reveal next."

Before I can ask what he means, he turns and pushes ahead, leading us to an exit, then down a set of stairs to the next level and the most horrific revelation yet.

A cavernous room, even larger than the holding area above. Hundreds of cages, many obscured by panels that have been set between them, dividing the room into semi-private segments. The stink is nauseating. Antoine offers us masks, but nobody takes one. As we progress farther into the room, I feel sorry that I didn't accept.

Some of the cages look like they've never been used, but many show signs of long-term occupancy, caked with ground-in filth. There are old blood and urine stains, scraps of hair everywhere. I spot the occasional fingernail or tooth. There are people at work in several cages, trying to clean them out. It's a job I wouldn't accept for the highest of wages.

"This smells almost as bad as that world of guts we visited,"

Shark mutters to Meera. She looks at him blankly. "Oh right. You weren't there. It was Sharmila."

"Nice to know you can't tell the difference between me and an Indian woman twice my age," Meera snaps. Shark winces — he's made the sort of error a woman never forgets or forgives.

"This is another holding pen," Antoine says. "But it's more than just a place to hold specimens. It's where we breed our own varieties, to increase our stock."

For a moment I don't catch his meaning. Then I stop dead. "You've been *breeding* werewolves?" I roar.

"The reproductive organs alter during transformation," Antoine explains, "but most specimens remain fertile. We always knew it was possible for them to breed, but we didn't follow up on that for many years. It's a delicate process. The pair have to be united at precisely the right moment, otherwise they rip each other apart. We tried artificial insemination, but the mothers refused to accept the young, killing them as they emerged from the womb. We could sedate and restrain them during the birthing process, of course, but it's much easier to —"

Losing my head completely, I take a swing at Antoine Horwitzer, intent on squeezing his brains out through his nose and ears, then stomping them into mincemeat.

Shark catches my fist. The suited leader of the Lambs ducks and recoils from me with a startled cry, while Shark restrains my trembling hand, staring at me coldly.

"Let go," I cry, angry tears trickling from my eyes.

"This isn't the time," he says quietly.

"I don't care. It's barbaric. I'm going to —"

"Kill him?" Shark hisses. "What will that achieve? He's just a pretty face in a suit. They'd replace him in an instant."

"But —"

"Remember our mission. Think about what's at stake. This guy's an ant. We can come after him later — and the rest of his foul kind. Right now we have bigger fish to fry. Don't lose track of the rabbit, Grubbs."

I struggle to break free. Then my brain kicks in and I relax. Shark releases me, but watches warily in case I make another break for Antoine, who's squinting at me nervously.

"You know your problem?" I snap at Shark. "You use too many metaphors. Ants, fish, and rabbits, all in the same breath. That's an abuse of the language."

Shark smiles. "I never was much good at school. Too busy reading about guns." He steps away, clearing the area between me and Antoine.

"Why?" I snarl. "Did you breed them to sell to circuses? To test your products on? Just to prove that you could?"

"We did it to experiment and learn," Antoine says. "The intake of regular specimens wasn't sufficient. We needed more. Also, by studying their growth from birth, we were able to find out more about them. We hoped the young might differ physically from their parents, that we could use their genes to develop a cure. There were many reasons, all of them honest and pure."

"No," I tell him. "Nothing about this is honest or pure. It's warped. If there's a hell, you've won yourself a one-way pass, you and all the rest of your bloody Lambs."

Antoine stifles a mocking yawn. I almost go for him again. Meera intervenes before things get out of hand.

"You didn't need to show us these pens," she says. "So I thank you for your open hospitality. It's hard for us to take in, but you knew we'd have difficulties. I imagine you struggled to adjust to the moral grey areas yourself at first."

"Absolutely." Antoine beams. "We're not monsters. We do these things to make the world a better place. I wasn't sure about the breeding program to begin with. I still harbor doubts. But we've learned so much, and the promise of learning more is tantalizing. Do we have the right to play God? Maybe not. But are we justified in trying to help people, to do all in our power to repay the faith of those who invest money and hope in our cause? With all my heart, I believe so."

Antoine smiles at me, trying to get me back on board. I don't return the gesture, but I don't glower at him either. Shark's right — this isn't the time to get into an argument. Antoine Horwitzer is our only link to Prae Athim. We have to keep him sweet or he might shut us out completely.

"Where are they?" I ask, nodding at the empty cages. "You said they vanished. What did you mean?"

Antoine nods, happy to be moving on to a less sensitive subject. "Prae was head of this unit for twenty-six years. She's been general director of the Lambs for nineteen of those. She worked on a number of private projects during her time in charge, commandeering staff and funds to conduct various experiments. She had a free reign for the past decade and a half.

"Under her guidance, the breeding program was accelerated. Bred specimens develop much faster than those that were once human — a newborn becomes an adult in three or four years, with an expected lifespan of ten to twelve years. We'd always bred in small numbers, but Prae increased the birth rate. Some people wondered why, but nobody challenged her. Prae was an exemplary director. We were sure she had good reasons for implementing the changes.

"A few months ago, she began making startling requests. She wanted to close down the programs and terminate all specimens."

"You mean kill all the werewolves?" Shark frowns.

"Yes. She said a new strain of the disease had developed and spread. We couldn't tell which were infected. If left to mutate and evolve, the strain might be passed to ordinary humans. She wanted to remove them to a secure area of her choosing, where they'd be safely disposed of.

"Nobody believed her." Antoine's face is grave. "There were too many holes in her story, no facts to support her theory. She argued fiercely, threatened to resign, called in every favor. But we weren't convinced. We insisted on more time to conduct our own experiments. Prae was allowed to continue in her post, but I was assigned to monitor her and approve her decisions.

"Just over six weeks ago, Prae Athim disappeared. She left work on a Thursday and nobody has seen her since. That night, operatives acting on her behalf subdued regular staff, tranquilized the specimens, removed them from their cells, and made off with them. We've no idea where they went. We've devoted all of our resources to tracking them down but so far . . . nothing."

Antoine smiles shakily. "I hoped she'd followed through on her plan to destroy the specimens. That would have been a tragic loss, but at least it would have meant we didn't have to worry about them. Now it seems my fears — that she had an ulterior motive — have been borne out. If some of them were sent to attack Dervish Grady, we're dealing with a far greater problem. We have to find the missing specimens as swiftly as possible. The consequences if we don't are staggering."

"I'm not that worried about the werewolves," Shark sniffs. "They're secondary to finding Prae Athim. I mean, how many are we talking about? A few dozen?"

Antoine laughs sharply. "You don't understand. I told you earlier — Prae Athim has worked in this unit for twenty-six years. But this is just one unit of many. We have bases on every continent and have been running similar programs in each. Prae didn't just take the specimens from this complex. She took them from *everywhere.* There's not one left."

Shark's expression darkens. "How many?" he croaks.

"I don't have an exact number to give," Antoine says. "Some of the projects were under Prae's personal supervision, and records have been deleted from our system. It's impossible to be accurate."

"Roughly," Shark growls.

Antoine gulps, then says quietly, so that we have to strain to hear, "Somewhere between six and seven hundred, give or take a few." And his smile, this time, is a pale ghost of a grin.

TIMAS ON THE JOB

✠ ✠ ✠

SIX or seven hundred werewolves on the loose, in the hands of a maniac most likely in league with Lord Loss. Nice! Demons rarely have time to kill many people because they can only stay on this world for a few minutes, while the window they crossed through remains open. But hundreds of werewolves, divided into groups of ten or twelve, set free in dozens of cities around the globe . . .

If each killed only five people, I make that three and a half thousand fatalities. But it's more likely they'd kill ten times that number, maybe more.

We're in Antoine's office on the eleventh floor. It used to be Prae Athim's. It's a large room, but with twelve of us it's a tight fit. Nobody's said anything since we came in. We've been looking through photos of the *specimens* that Antoine gave us, studying the data that he has on file.

I know from my own brush with lycanthropy that werewolves are strong and fast. I felt like an Olympic athlete when it was my time of turning. But I'm still seriously freaked by what I'm reading. I never knew they were *this* advanced.

I shouldn't let it matter. The Shadow must remain the priority. If it succeeds in uniting the demon masses and breaking through, the world will fall. The damage a pack of escaped werewolves might cause is nothing in comparison.

But how can I ignore the possibility of tens of thousands of deaths? Beranabus could. He's half-demon and has spent hundreds of years subduing his human impulses. We're statistics to him. He'd take the line that a few thousand lives don't make much difference in the grand scheme of things, that we have to focus on the millions and billions — *real* numbers.

I can't do that. Even if we find out that the attack in Carcery Vale has nothing to do with the demon assault at the hospital, that Prae Athim isn't working with Lord Loss, I have to try and stop her. I won't let thousands of people die if I can prevent it. Especially not when the killers are relatives of mine.

Perhaps crazily, I still think of the werewolves as kin, even those bred in cages. They're part of the Grady clan. That makes it personal.

"We have to find them," I blurt out, without meaning to. All heads in the office bob up and everybody stares at me. I'm sitting by one of the large windows, the city spread out behind me. Any of the people on the streets, eleven floors down, could fall victim to the werewolves if Prae Athim unleashes them.

"We have to stop this." I get to my feet, discarding the photos I'd been mutely studying.

"Maybe there's nothing to stop," Meera says unconvincingly. "Maybe Prae was telling the truth about a new disease and took them to dispose of safely. Perhaps the few who were sent to attack Dervish were simply being used to settle an old score, and were then executed along with the rest."

"Bull!" Shark snorts. "If she'd wanted to kill them, she'd have slaughtered them in their cages. It would have been a lot simpler than smuggling them out."

"Probably," Meera sighs. "I was just saying *maybe* . . ."

"What will she do with them?" Marian asks.

"I guess she'll drop them off in a city somewhere," Shark replies. "Let them run wild. Maybe collect them at the end and take them on somewhere else."

"But why?" Marian frowns. "Why not build bombs, poison a city's water supply or develop chemical weapons? Hijacking hundreds of werewolves to use as crazed assassins . . . it's like something out of a *Batman* comic!"

"Crazy people don't think the way we do," Meera says glumly. "They have all sorts of warped ideas and plans, and if they gain enough power, they get to inflict their mad schemes on others."

"Like Davida Haym in Slawter," I note.

"There's another possibility," Terry says. "She might have done this for humane reasons. Maybe she suffered a moral crisis. Decided they'd been mistreating these creatures. Took them somewhere isolated, to set them free."

"Unlikely," Antoine says with a cynical smile. "Her people

killed seventeen of our staff during the breakouts. Many more were seriously injured. Hardly the work of a good samaritan."

"I've seen fanatics who think animals are nobler than humans," Terry says. "They'd happily kill a human to save a dog or cat from abuse."

"Prae Athim isn't an animal rights activist," Antoine says firmly. "I refuse to entertain the notion that she did this to free the specimens, that she stood waving them off as they returned to the wilds, happy tears in her eyes."

"He's right," Shark says. "We have to assume this was done with the intent of creating maximum havoc."

"So let's track her down and stop her," I snarl. "We can't just sit here and talk about it. We have to . . . to . . ." I throw my hands up, frustrated.

"We all know how you feel," Meera says sympathetically. "But until she makes a move, there's nothing we can do. The world's a big place. You could hide seven hundred werewolves just about anywhere. We can't —"

"I could find them," Timas interrupts. "If I had access to your mainframe," he adds, smiling at Antoine.

"I told you — the records have been wiped," Antoine scowls.

"It's virtually impossible to wipe a mainframe completely clean," Timas says. "That's one of the reasons I was surprised you still used one. I can perform at the very least a partial restore."

"We've had experts working on it for the last six weeks," Antoine says sharply.

"I'm sure you've employed some of the best people in the business," Timas says earnestly. "But I'm the *very* best."

"Even assuming you could restore it," Shark rumbles, "how would that help us? She's unlikely to have outlined her secret plans on a work computer."

"You can't move that many bodies around without leaving a trail," Timas says. "If I find out more about the creatures, I can use that information to fish for clues on the Web."

"What do you mean?" Shark asks.

"They didn't take the cages," Timas notes. "That means they transported them in cages of their own. Once I know what the cages are made from, I can search for companies who specialize in this type of construction and find out if they've filled any large orders recently. If they have, I'll learn where they delivered the cages to.

"If I can determine how the werewolves were tranquilized, I can track the drugs back to where they were manufactured, then trace them through delivery records.

"How did they transport the creatures — airplanes, articulated trucks, trains, boats? I'm assuming they moved at least some of them across international borders. There will be a trail of red tape, no matter how surreptitiously they went about it. I've followed such trails before and enjoyed a large measure of success.

"Do you want me to continue explaining or shall I get started?" Timas addresses this question to Antoine Horwitzer.

Antoine's torn. "Is he really that good?" he asks Shark.

"Yes."

"If he can do what he says . . . he will have access to confidential information. He'll have to sign a privacy clause. We need absolute affirmation that he'd never reveal —"

"You present the forms, he'll sign them," Shark cuts in.

Antoine struggles with the idea for a couple of seconds, then sighs. "Very well. I'll log you in and provide you with the relevant security codes."

"No need," Timas says, sliding into Antoine's plush leather chair. "I can crack them. The exercise will serve as a useful warm-up."

"How long will it take?" Shark asks as Timas's fingers dance across the keyboard.

"A few days, I imagine," Timas replies absently. "Quicker if we get a lucky break. Longer if she's hidden her trail artfully. I'll need complete privacy. And my equipment from the helicopter."

"I'll have it sent down," Shark says, and ushers us out.

"Perhaps I should stay and keep an eye on him," Antoine says nervously.

"No chance," Shark responds firmly, and pushes out the suave chief executive, ignoring his spluttering protests.

Some of the rooms on the uppermost floor have beds, or couches that pull out into sleeping cots. Members of the higher echelon move around a lot between buildings owned by the Lambs. Given the secretive nature of their business, they often prefer to stay onsite rather than check into hotels.

I'm sharing a room with Spenser and James. They don't speak to me much. They know I'm part of Beranabus's world of magic and demons, but they've had little first-hand experience of that. They find it hard to think of me as anything other than an especially large but otherwise unremarkable teenager. I'm not too bothered. I find most of their conversation pretty boring — weapons, planes, helicopters, war, battle tactics. I'm happy to be excluded.

I spend my spare time experimenting, testing my powers. I don't know how much I'm capable of doing on this world, in the absence of magical energy. I want to find out what my limits are, so as not to exceed them and leave myself exposed.

I'm pretty good at moving objects. Size doesn't seem to matter — I can slide a heavy oak wardrobe across the floor as easily as a telephone. I spend a couple of hours moving things around. I'm pretty beat by the end, and not back to full health until the next morning. It's reassuring that I can recharge, but worrying that it takes so long once I've been drained.

Other maneuvers are more demanding. I can heighten my senses — to eavesdrop on a conversation, or view a scene from a few miles away — but that takes a lot of effort and quickly eats into my resources. I can't change shape, but I can make myself partially invisible for a very short time. I can create fire and freeze objects, but again those demand a lot of me. I can shoot off several bolts of magical energy, but I'm good for nothing for hours afterwards.

There are all sorts of compensating spells that I could make use of if I knew them. But I refused to dabble in magic when I lived with Dervish and I didn't need spells in the Demonata universe — if a spell was required there, Beranabus took care of it. He wasn't interested in training Kernel or me, just in using us to bully and kill demons.

I wish I'd demanded more of Beranabus and Dervish. Mages can do a lot with a few subtle spells. As a magician I could do even more. I get Meera to teach me some simple incantations, but we don't have time to cover much ground.

I worry about my uncle constantly. What's he doing? Where is he? Time moves differently in the other universe, usually faster or slower than here. Years might have passed for him, or only minutes. Is he alive or dead? I've no way of knowing. Beranabus taught me how to open windows, so I could go and find them. But I couldn't guarantee how long that would take.

I have to remain here until our mission's over. I'm the reason the others are involved, the one who vowed to track down Prae Athim and uncover the truth. I can't cut out early. That would be the selfish act of a child, which I'm not. I'm a Disciple. We see things through to the end. No matter how scared and alone we feel.

Four days pass. Everyone's impatient for news, but Timas refuses to provide us with partial updates. On the few occasions that Shark barges into Antoine's office and demands answers, the reply is always the same. "I'll summon you promptly when I've concluded my investigations."

Timas finally reaches that conclusion shortly before dawn on the fifth day. Shark hammers on our door, waking us all, then sticks his head in and shouts, "The office! Now!"

Five minutes later we're all huddled around Timas and his computers. We're bleary-eyed, hair all over the place, typical early morning messes. Except Timas. As far as I know, he's worked almost nonstop since I last saw him, sleeping only two or three hours a night. But he looks as perky as an actor in a TV commercial.

"I've found them," he says without any preliminaries. "They're on an island. It has no official name, but the Lambs nicknamed it Wolf Island. Prae Athim purchased it through a fifth-generation contact several years ago."

"What's a fifth-generation contact?" I ask.

"A contact of a contact of a contact of a contact of a contact," Timas intones. "She conducts most of her business that way, making it almost impossible to trace anything back to her personally. *Almost,*" he repeats with a justifiably smug smile.

"Where's the island?" Shark grunts.

Timas passes him a stapled printout of about twenty pages, then hands copies around to the rest of us. The small sheaf is crammed with all sorts of info about the island, its history, dimensions, wildlife, plant life, natural formations. There are several maps, most of the island, but also of the surrounding waters, noting currents, depth, temperatures, sea life.

"They've built a base," Timas points out. "Page nine. They constructed it on the island's largest crag, so they need only face an assault from one direction if the werewolves get out of control. That extra measure wasn't a necessity — the fortifications are sound, with more than six separate security systems in place, powered by a variety of independent generators. The werewolves might have the run of the island, but the people inside the compound are quite —"

"The beasts are running free?" Shark interrupts.

"Yes. That's on page four. They were set loose once delivered to the island, though they can be recaptured, singly or in small groups, using a variety of equipment provided for such a purpose."

"Maybe Terry was right," Meera says dubiously. "Perhaps Prae took them there to let them live naturally."

"I think not," Timas purrs, "and would refer you to page fourteen, appendix Bii, in support of my opinion."

Antoine and a few of the others flick forward. Shark tosses his copy of the report aside and snaps, "Don't play games. Just tell us."

"No games," Timas says mildly. "The appendix outlines everything concisely. But if you would prefer an oral report . . ."

"I would," Shark snarls.

"No!" Antoine gasps, turning a shade paler beneath his tan. He must be a speed-reader because he's already flicking from page fourteen to fifteen, eyes scanning the lines superfast. "This can't be right. I would have known."

"The figures are accurate," Timas says. "Nothing is speculative." He faces Shark. "A third have been genetically, surgically, and electronically modified by Prae Athim and her team. She found a way to corrupt their metabolisms. This allowed her to do two things. First, using steroids, implants, and a variety of drugs, she created faster, stronger animals. Second, by operating on their brains and using other implants, she was able to train them."

"They can't survive at those levels," Antoine says, glancing up from his report. "Their bodies can't hold, not subjected to such degrees of abuse."

"Their long-term prospects are grim," Timas agrees. "But they can last a few years, or so the scientists believe."

"What have they been trained to do?" Shark asks.

"Nothing too complex," Timas says. "They can hunt in small groups, in pursuit of predefined targets — like hounds, they can be given a person's scent. They're not as reliable as hounds. In a crowded environment they might be distracted and chase others instead. And they'll turn on their handlers afterwards unless subdued. But that's a huge step forward."

"I'd no idea she'd advanced to such a stage," Antoine whispers. "We've been trying to install control mechanisms for decades. We could have done so much good if we'd known about this. We still could."

"The Lambs are finished," Shark says, "at least as far as werewolves are concerned. Do you really think people will trust you with their young once word of this gets out? And it will — have no doubt about that."

"You're right," Antoine sighs. "But those on the island are still alive. If we can bring them back under our authority and follow up on these incredible breakthroughs . . ."

"You're assuming we'll leave any of them alive," Shark laughs brutally. Before Antoine can react to that, he says to

Timas, "What's the best way to hit them? Do we need more troops?"

Timas purses his lips. "If the original implants had been left intact, we could have electronically disabled them from the air. But they were all secretly removed or rendered inactive prior to the abduction. The safest way would be to blanket-bomb the island."

"No!" I cry. "You can't just kill them. They were human once."

"They're not anymore," Shark shrugs.

"I won't let you," I growl.

"You can't stop me," he says blankly.

"Actually, I can." I raise a hand and let little forks of blue lightning crackle between my fingertips. Shark squints at me, taking my measure.

"He'd whup you," Meera says to Shark. "He's a magician. You wouldn't stand a chance."

"Probably not." Shark grimaces. "Besides, I don't trust flyboys and their damn guided missiles. They could level the compound by accident, and we need Prae alive. Options, Timas?"

"Go as we are." He holds up his copy of the report, flicks to near the end, and taps the page. "There are very few guards. It's mostly scientists and medics. If we just hit the compound, we can drop in and make a neat job of it."

"You're sure?" Shark asks.

"Absolutely," Timas says. "I can provide you with a complete breakdown of the odds if you wish."

"No need," Shark smiles. "Twelve it is."

"Thirteen," Antoine corrects him.

Shark laughs. "You're not serious."

"Never more so. I'm coming."

"You're not," Shark says, his smile disappearing. "This is a job for soldiers and Disciples."

"I won't pretend to be an action hero," Antoine says with quiet dignity. "I'm not your equal in matters such as these. But I'm coming regardless. I run this operation now. I'm not sure what you want with Prae, but if you don't kill her, I plan to bring her to justice. And there's the matter of the specimens. They have to be returned. Or perhaps we can continue our work on the island. I need to undertake a study before I make a proposal to the board."

"You can do that later," Meera says. "Let us go in, shut down Prae's operation, and take control of the situation. You can fly in after we're finished and —"

"You don't understand!" Antoine shouts, losing his temper for the first time. His jaw trembles as he glares at us. "This happened on *my* watch. I was supposed to control her. There have already been calls for my head. I'm hanging on to this job by my fingernails. If the board of governors finds out about this island and that I let you waltz in unrestricted and unmonitored . . ."

Antoine looks appealingly at Shark. "I need to come with you. And it won't be a one-way favor. I can help. I know Prae, her people, the specimens. I can advise and caution if necessary."

"It'd be dangerous," Shark says. "If you come, you're on your own. Nobody will risk their life to save yours."

"In this business, you never expect anyone to be helpful." Antoine smirks, in command of his temper again. "Do I have time to pack a few things?"

"No," Shark snorts, and marches out of the office. The rest of us follow him up the stairs to where the helicopter is waiting, and off we set for Wolf Island. *Arooooo!*

PREY

✠ ✠ ✠

WE manage to squeeze into the Farrier Harrier, even though it isn't meant to hold more than twelve. We fly all day, Shark and James taking turns to pilot. We set down a couple of times to refuel, eat, and stretch our legs. Stop at dusk for dinner at an army base, then continue through the night. I catch a few hours of sleep, using a sleeping spell to drop off.

We make our final stop shortly after nine in the morning. Breakfast, a walk, exercise. Then Shark talks us through our plans. We scour maps of the compound, Shark highlighting our route and alternatives in case we run into problems. It's pretty simple — break in, grab Prae Athim, secure the area around her office and interrogate her there, or else abduct her and make a quick getaway.

Meera doesn't suggest a polite approach this time. Prae Athim is way out of control. Subtlety won't work on Wolf Island.

Shark finishes by asking for any last-minute comments or inquiries. Antoine sheepishly raises a hand. "Will you try not to cause unnecessary damage? Some of the equipment is very expensive. If we can recycle it later, we can recoup some of the costs of this debacle."

Shark glares at Antoine. "If we come through this and I receive an invoice for wreckages, I'll find you, string you upside down, and make you eat your own brains before I kill you. Understand?"

Antoine flushes. "I was only —"

"Be quiet," Meera snaps.

Antoine pouts, but shuts up. Shark casts an eye around. "Last chance to back out. Anyone?" Seven of the nine soldiers promptly raise their hands. "You should be in a sitcom," Shark jeers, then claps his hands together loudly and stands. "Let's go!"

Back on the helicopter. Within minutes we're over open water. No retreating now. We're in this to the bitter, bloody end.

✠ The island is one of many in the area, all deserted, most uninhabitable. This is one of the largest. A lot of grass, wildflowers, trees. We spot the werewolves as we skim the treetops. Spread across the island in small groups, most relaxing, some eating (I don't think much of the natural wildlife exists there anymore), a few fighting. Mutated, vicious, hairy monstrosities, all fangs, claws, and muscles. Some howl at us as we pass overhead, though we can't hear them over the roar of the blades.

The wolf within me tries to force its way to the surface, howling silently in reply to its warped brethren. I'm one of the cursed Gradys. I should have turned into a werewolf. I only survived because I'm a magician. My magic self wrestled with my wolfen side and triumphed. But I've never rid myself of the wolf, only driven it down deep inside.

I don't have any difficulty keeping my wolfish instincts in check, but I'm surprised to find that a part of me doesn't want to remain in control. I'm excited by the creatures running free beneath us. Life would be much simpler if I abandoned my humanity and ran wild with them, gave myself over to animalistic pleasures, free of the burdens of duty and responsibility.

I'm envious of my twisted relatives, but sad for them too. Because I know their freedom is temporary. If it all goes wrong and Prae Athim turns the tables on us, she'll use these *specimens* for her own sick ends. But life won't be much better for them if we succeed. Antoine Horwitzer will take over, pick the werewolves off one by one, slice them open, and carry out all manner of unpleasant experiments.

I'm so glad Gret and Bill-E aren't down there. In a weird way I'd rather they were dead than captive on this island. Better to be out of life entirely than struggle through it as a tormented, hopeless, inhuman victim.

The others are studying the werewolves with a mixture of curiosity and loathing. They have no ties to these unfortunate mutants. They view them simply as enemies. If our plan works, we should have no dealings with the werewolves. But if complications set in, the soliders might find themselves up against the killer beasts, and in that case they'll have to be ruthless.

Antoine is the only one not awed by the spectacle. He stole a quick glance at the werewolves when we hit the island's edge, then closed his eyes, dug rosary beads out of a pocket, and began to pray. I hadn't pegged him as a religious type, but when I think about it, it makes sense. After all, the Lambs named themselves after a biblical quote.

My stomach clenches and I almost throw up. It's the werewolf, fighting to free itself. I stop staring at Antoine and focus on driving the wolf back inside. It retreats reluctantly and I feel sorry for it. If I could let it loose for a while, somewhere it couldn't cause damage, I would, just to give it a taste of freedom.

The compound walls come into sight. I was expecting a fence, but there isn't one, only a long wall of high, thick, metal panels. Lots of werewolves are gathered by the wall, hurling themselves at it, clawing its smooth grey surface, howling at those inside, the stench of human flesh thick in their nostrils. (The stench is also thick in mine. My lips tremble and I am careful not to drool.)

As we approach the wall I catch my first glimpse of the compound. It's built on the extended tip of the island, surrounded on three sides by cliffs and water. The werewolves have only one route of attack. Even if they could swim (Antoine told us they can't), they'd struggle to climb the sheer cliffs, despite their claws.

The compound's nothing special. A series of grey, drab buildings with flat aluminium roofs. There are lots of grooves in the ground, which Timas points out, speaking through the microphone on his headset.

"They use the grooves to slot the walls into place," he explains. "An ingenious system. Just lay the grooves, then slide the panels around and click them together. Makes it easy to shuffle the rooms and alter the layout."

"Those walls can't be sturdy," Shark grunts.

"They are," Timas insists. "Designed to withstand anything nature can throw at them. The architects couldn't take chances, not with hundreds of werewolves lying in wait on the other side."

There's a landing pad inside the main wall, to the left. A single helicopter stands idle. There are several motorboats stored under tarpaulins at either side of the crag, rope ladders stacked beside them. In the event of an evacuation, that's how the staff would leave, lowering the boats and climbing down into them.

Guards spill out of the nearest building as we touch down, cocking rifles and pistols. One roars through a megaphone, commanding us to come out unarmed.

"This is it!" Shark yells, brandishing his handguns. "Don't kill if you can help it, but don't show too much mercy either. These guys knew what they were signing up for. They've already murdered seventeen people. They'll rip us to shreds if we give them the chance."

He rolls out and across the ground, leaps to his feet, and opens fire, supported instantly by his team, even Timas, wielding a high-tech weapon that provides him with all sorts of fascinating feedback.

Meera and I share a worried glance, then slide out after the others onto the bullet-riddled Tarmac, leaving James and Marian to guard the helicopter. Antoine stumbles out after us, still praying, crouched low, sweat staining the collar of his otherwise spotless shirt.

The air is ablaze with gunfire. A number of guards are already lying wounded or dead. Others are firing wildly. It's a simple matter for the well-trained members of Shark's squad to pick them off.

The last few, realizing the futility of their position, discard their weapons and thrust their hands into the air. The gunfire ceases. Leo darts forward and makes them lie down, then handcuffs their wrists and ankles. While he's doing that, the other soldiers advance to the open door and surround it. When Leo joins them, Shark holds up three fingers and counts down. Liam and Terry burst through, laying down a spray of advance fire. In pairs, the rest of the team follow them in. Meera and I bring up the rear, Antoine and Pip ahead of us. The bloodshed sickens me. I don't mind slaughtering demons, but these are *people.* It's not right. I know we have no choice, that these guys are murderers, but still . . .

Cool inside. Air-conditioned. Brightly lit. Liam and Terry are already at the end of the room and halfway through the door to the next room or corridor. No sign of anybody else. These are living quarters. Bunks, cabinets, racks for clothes, photos of models and relatives pinned to the walls. Those we hit outside must have been relaxing. They wouldn't have been expecting an attack. I wish they hadn't reacted so swiftly. If we'd caught them in here, we wouldn't have had to kill so many.

"You OK?" Meera asks as we wait for the call to advance.

"Not really," I groan.

"I know it's hard," she says quietly. "Try not to think of them as humans but as demonic assistants."

"But they probably know nothing about the Demonata," I protest.

"They knew about the seventeen Lambs they killed," Meera snaps. "These aren't innocents."

"But they're still people. I don't feel comfortable killing like this."

Meera smiles wanly. "That's a good thing. Try and hold on to that attitude. The world's packed with too many trigger-happy goons."

"Like Shark?" I grin shakily.

Meera's face puckers into something between a scowl and a smirk. Before she can answer, one of the soldiers — I think it's Spenser — shouts affirmatively, and we're moving forward again, farther into the heart of the compound.

✠ We don't encounter much resistance. The occasional guard or two. We're able to overpower most of them and leave them handcuffed, alive. We only face one real obstacle, when several guards block a long corridor and fill it with furniture. They have a great vantage point. If we try to rush them, we'll be cut down before we get halfway. But Shark isn't fazed. He calls Pip forward. She studies the piled-up furniture, makes a few calculations, then takes off her back-pack and roots through it. Produces a small round object. It looks like a thick CD.

"Who's good with Frisbees?" Pip asks.

"Here," Liam says. He takes the disc, aims, then glances at Pip. "Do I need to press anything?"

"No. But if you don't throw it quickly, you'll lose an arm."

Liam yelps, then sends the disc skimming down the corridor. It hits the mound of furniture near the base and explodes on contact. The desks, chairs, and cabinets fly backwards, obliterating the guards behind them. We're on the scene seconds later, Shark's troops handcuffing any survivors. Stephen bends over a seriously wounded man. Starts to cuff him, then pauses, studies his injuries, sets him down, and presses the barrel of his gun to the man's head. I look away but I can't drown out the retort of the muffled shot.

We push on, the air thick with the stench of scorched wood, blood, and whatever was in Pip's bomb. Antoine's still praying. I almost feel like joining in.

The corridors and rooms all look the same to me, but the soldiers know exactly where they're going. A couple of minutes later, we're at the door of Prae Athim's office. There are no markings to confirm that, but Timas is certain. He steps ahead of us and raps softly. "Knock, knock," he calls. "Anybody home?"

He pushes the door open and we spill in.

A large room. Grey walls. Harsh fluorescent lights. A single bed. A black, high-backed leather chair in the center of the floor. Someone's sitting in it, facing away from us. I can only see the person's lower legs, but I'm sure it's Prae Athim.

"Hey!" Shark barks. No answer. He looks at us. Nods at Pip to advance and check for explosives. She creeps forward, skirting the chair, pistol trained on the person in it. As she angles to the front, she pauses, face crinkling. Shaking her head, she stoops, checks the chair for wires and devices, then puts her hand on one of the arms and swivels it around.

I was right. It's Prae Athim. But, to my bewilderment, she's strapped down, a strip of tape across her mouth, incapable of movement or sound.

We gape at the sight. Prae Athim glares at us. Shark gulps, then strides forward and grabs hold of one end of the tape over her mouth. Before he can tear it free, somebody shouts a weird word. Whipping round, I spot Antoine Horwitzer, arms wide, grinning crazily. He yells a couple more words and the air shimmers behind him. Too late, I realize the nature of the trap we've walked into. I start to roar a warning, but the window opens before I can.

It's an enormous dark window. As I stare at it, horrified, a deformed, miserable-looking creature slithers through. It has the general shape of a woman, but her flesh is bubbling with sores and boils. Pus and blood seep from wounds all over her body. There's a rancid stink. The eyes are swimming bowls of madness in a ruined face. The mouth is a jagged gash. I know who this abomination is from Dervish's description, but I would have recognized her anyway.

"Hello, Grubbs," the thing that was once Juni Swan gurgles. "Have you missed me?"

There's no time to answer. Right behind Juni, dozens of guards file in three abreast, weapons cradled to their chests. Spreading out, they take aim. Before a stunned Shark and his team can react, an officer bellows a command and the air around us is ripped apart by a lethal hail of bullets.

OPEN SEASON

✠ ✠ ✠

WITHOUT magic we'd have perished instantly. But magical energy streams through the window, as it always does when a passageway between universes is opened. Tapping into that instinctively, I throw up a barrier between us and the guards. The bullets mushroom against it and drop harmlessly to the floor. As more troops flood into the room, I strengthen the barrier and start thinking about ways to make it a one-way shield, so that we can fire at them.

Before I can do that, Juni barks a short command. The window pulses, then snaps out of existence. The flow of magic stops, and though a strong residue is left in the air, I now have to work off a dwindling supply. Altering the shield would take a lot out of me. Too much.

"How long can you hold that?" Shark yells.

"A couple of minutes," I guess.

"Pip!" he roars.

"On it," she mutters, darting to the rear of the wall to my right. There's a corridor on the other side that bypasses the section of the building we came through. Shark was keeping it in reserve in case we needed an escape route.

As Meera frees Prae Athim, the guards on the other side of the shield part to allow Juni Swan and a smirking Antoine Horwitzer to advance. They come to within a couple of inches of the barrier. Juni smiles crookedly at the shield, then at me.

"Nice work, Grubbs," she gurgles, her voice a hoarse mockery of what it once was. "But what more can you do in the absence of demonic energy?"

"As much as you," I snarl.

"Possibly," she chuckles. "But I don't have to do anything. Not with so many finely armed humans to depend on."

"Did you pay them much?" Shark sneers.

"Antoine recruited them on my behalf," she says.

"Most humans have a price," Antoine chuckles. "I've always been adept at calculating such sums."

"I'll have your head for this, Horwitzer!" Prae Athim screams, ripping the tape from her mouth and thrusting a finger at Antoine. "You're finished!"

"Don't be silly," he coos. "You can't do anything to me. Your reign has come to its natural end. I run the Lambs now."

"Why this way?" she snarls. "You were always power-hungry, but you'd have squeezed me out eventually. Why betray us to monstrous fiends like this?"

"Careful," Juni growls. "You don't want to hurt my feelings."

"It's the dawn of a new age." Antoine smiles. "Our associates can provide us with the cure for lycanthropy, but that's only the tip of the iceberg. I was never much interested in that side of the business. While you were wasting money on werewolves, I was busy making it in other fields. We're already a major force, but when we move into areas of supernatural energy, we'll be in a class of our own."

"I'm ready," Pip calls.

"Give us a minute," Shark says, then squares up to Juni. "I never liked you. When you were Beranabus's assistant, all you ever did was complain. You're weak and petty, a disgrace to the Disciples."

Juni stares impassively at Shark. "Insult me all you like. You'll be dead soon. We'll see who's laughing then." She looks around and spots Meera. Her smile blossoms again. "You had a lucky escape in Carcery Vale. You won't get away this time."

"You were in the Vale?" Meera frowns.

"Of course," Juni says. "I was outside. I was sorely tempted to break into the cellar. I could smell the three of you and I knew Dervish was incapacitated. But my master warned me to be wary of Bec . . . of the Kah-Gash."

"So that's what this is about," I snarl, our suspicions — that the attacks were the work of Lord Loss and the Shadow — confirmed. "You want the Kah-Gash."

"Obviously," Juni sniffs. "Did you think my master would stand by and let you wield the most powerful weapon ever known? That he'd wait for you to learn how to use it, so you could destroy our universe?"

"But why try to kill us?" I frown. "The werewolves could have ripped Bec to pieces. Surely you need her — and me — alive."

"Not at all," Juni sneers. "Our new master deals in death. I'm proof of that — he released my soul and let me walk among the living again. I'm here to harvest your spirit, just as I would have harvested Bec's if she'd been killed. It's simpler to let others do our dirty work, then steal your parts of the Kah-Gash as you perish. We weren't sure how powerful you might be, so —" She gasps, clutches her chest, and bends over. Takes several breaths, then stands again.

"You don't look too healthy," I laugh wickedly.

"This body won't last long," she says. "A shell for my soul to inhabit. I'll return to death soon, and return gladly. But rest assured, your uncle's in far worse shape. I saw him just before I came here."

I stiffen fearfully. "You're lying."

"No," she says. "He was on a pleasure cruiser, although he didn't seem to be getting much pleasure out of it. My new master decided to deal with Bec personally, and since Dervish and Beranabus were with her, they're dead now, or will be soon. Just like you when your barrier crumbles."

I start to press her for more information, but Shark grips my arm. "We've learned all we need to know. Time to get out of here."

"But Dervish —" I cry.

"— will have to look after himself," Shark finishes. He yells at Pip, "Now!"

There's a small explosion. As the dust clears, Pip slips through a hole in the wall and the others push after her. I glance at Juni. She's smiling.

"My team will catch up with you outside," she says. "And I've another surprise lined up. I'll wait here. I don't need to be too close when you die."

"Any last words for the board, Prae?" Antoine asks. She hits him with some of the foulest insults I've ever heard, but he doesn't even blink. He's loving this. It would be easy to blame myself for not seeing through him before, but he conned us all. Besides, there's no time for self-blame. If we reach the helicopter before Juni's soldiers, we might get out of here. We're not finished yet — if we're fast.

"Later!" I snap at Juni, locking gazes with her, letting her see how serious I am. I mean to kill her the next time we meet, as slowly and painfully as possible.

Juni only laughs with mad delight at the threat, then waves mockingly. "Run, run as fast as you can, but I'll catch you, little ginger-haired man."

"Grubbs!" Shark shouts. He's standing by the hole in the wall. Everyone's gone through except him and Meera.

I hold Juni's gaze one last second, then turn my back on the mutant and her troops, and dive for safety. As I squeeze through the hole, I hear the sounds of dozens of feet scuffling out of the room as the soldiers set off to intercept us.

The race is on.

✠ ✠ ✠

✠ Running as fast as we can, Timas in the lead. He's playing with the tiny console on his gun as he runs. He looks the least worried of us all.

"I can't believe you trusted that charlatan," Prae Athim pants, glancing over her shoulder at me.

"He told us you stole the werewolves," I growl. "Based on your previous threat to kidnap Bill-E and me, why wouldn't we believe him?"

"Anyway, he worked for *you*," Meera chips in. "Why didn't you see this coming?"

"Enough!" Shark huffs as Prae bristles. "If they catch us before we make it outside, it doesn't matter who's to blame — we'll all be crapping bullets."

We push on in silence. I'm finding it difficult to keep up. Although I'm fit, I'm used to operating on magic. It's been a long time since I worked up a sweat. I'm out of practice.

I can hear Juni's guards, their cries to one another. They're keeping pace with us but can't break through. We have a slight advantage, but it's *very* slight. And if they make it to the yard before us, or if there are more out there already . . .

The corridor feels much longer than it appeared on the map. I start to think we're in a maze, doomed to wander in circles until we run into Juni's troops and are mowed down. I consider using magic to guide us out. But that would be a waste of energy. I have to hold it back. Use it only when the situation is truly desperate. Which probably won't be long.

Timas bursts through a door and sunlight streams in. Finding an extra burst of speed, we hurry through, out into the yard where we fought with the first group of guards. It's deserted except for James and Marian in the Farrier Harrier. As soon as they see us, James fires the engines up to full, readying the helicopter for a swift getaway.

We race for the chopper. I picture myself clambering to safety along with everybody else. We lift off, zip out over the water, laughing at our narrow escape, leaving Juni behind to curse and rant. But in my heart I know it won't be that easy. And sure enough, before we've taken six strides, Juni's troops hit the scene and the gunfire starts.

Pip LeMat is ahead of everyone, having overtaken Timas, so she should have been the safest. But she's the first to catch a spray of bullets. She hits the ground hard and doesn't move, blood already seeping from beneath her still form.

Shark and the others spin 180 degrees, even as Pip is falling, and open up with their own weapons. "Run!" Shark yells at Meera and me. "Get out of here. We'll cover you."

I start to protest, but Meera pushes me forward. "Don't argue!" she shouts.

"We can't just leave them," I cry as half of Terry's head disappears. He remains standing a moment, then slumps forward. Leo takes a hit to the shoulder. He roars with pain, but continues to return fire. Prae Athim grabs Terry's gun and pitches in with the others, screaming manically.

"You heard what Juni said," Meera snarls. "You're the only

one who matters. If she gets her hands on you, we're done for."

"Like we're not already!" I shriek.

"All the rest of us have to worry about is death," Meera says. "From what Juni said, that's only the start for you. If the Shadow gets your piece of the Kah-Gash . . ."

I stare at her helplessly. I know she's right, but these soldiers have become our friends. We can't simply abandon them.

"A barrier," I wheeze. "We can construct a shield and —"

Meera slaps me hard. "Get in that helicopter or they'll have died for nothing."

I stare at her numbly, then lurch forward. Bullets rip up the ground close by my feet, but I don't flinch. My eyes are filling with tears. I don't want to escape if the cost is losing Shark and his team, but Meera's right. We have no choice. The Kah-Gash mustn't fall into the Shadow's hands.

I'm about halfway to the Farrier Harrier when a horn blares, overriding the noise of the helicopter and guns. I shouldn't stop, but I can't help myself. Pausing, I glance back and see Juni's men retreating into the building. At least a dozen have been killed or are lying wounded. But everyone else is ducking out of sight.

Shark was crouched low, but now he stands and stares after the departing troops. He's as confused as I am. Then, as the squeal of the horn dies away, we hear something else. A grinding noise coming from the outer wall of the compound.

We whirl as one, just in time to see the wall split in several places. We should have seen this coming. Timas told us, when he was explaining about the grooves in the ground.

Everything here is built out of metal panels that can be swiftly slid together — or just as easily slid apart.

As we watch with a sickening sense of helplessness, panels roll back, leaving gaping holes in the wall. Seconds later I spot the first werewolf sniffing at the gap. Then it catches our scent and bounds ahead, followed by dozens more. They converge on us like giant locusts, screeching, howling, free at last to attack and kill.

RUNNING THE GAUNTLET

✠ ✠ ✠

THE helicopter!" Shark roars, leading the break for our only hope of survival. We pound after him, but I see within seconds that we haven't a snowman in hell's chance. The werewolves are closer to the helicopter than we are, and they can run faster.

Alert to the danger, James starts to take his Farrier Harrier up, out of the reach of the onrushing werewolves. But he's not quick enough. One of the larger beasts takes a running leap and grabs hold of the skid on the pilot's side. Marian levels her gun at it, but the weight of the werewolf causes the helicopter to lurch and she's jolted off target. The werewolf hauls itself up onto the skid and drives its fists and head through the pilot's window. It locks its jaws on James's terror-stricken face and savages him.

James battles hopelessly against the werewolf, tries to thrash free, fails, then goes limp. The helicopter spins out of control, swishes left then right, then banks and smashes into the compound wall. The rotors snap off with an ear-splitting squeal. The blood-spattered glass shatters and the body of the helicopter buckles inwards. But it doesn't explode like I expect it to.

I spot a shaken, bloodied Marian struggling from the remains of the wreckage. Three werewolves jump her while she's half out of the helicopter. They drive her back inside and finish her off, fighting over the scraps.

The first werewolf is on us before we can feel any pity for James and Marian. Shark takes careful aim and fires a bullet through the center of its head. Then he changes direction and darts for the helicopter that was already here when we arrived. He bellows at us to follow.

Werewolves quickly fill the area around us. Shark and his remaining soldiers fire at them freely, wounding, maiming, killing. I can't work up any sympathy for my unfortunate relatives. It's them or us now.

Timas stoops over Pip's body as we pass, swiftly loosens her backpack, and burrows through it as he runs, whistling casually. He picks out a device, smiles, shakes his head, and carefully replaces it. Never drops his pace, keeping up with the rest of us even though he's not concentrating.

Some of the werewolves are distracted by the stranded, wounded survivors of Juni's forces — easy pickings. The ground between us and the helicopter partially clears. Shark and his team focus their fire on those who remain in our way, opening a path. Hope flares within me. The despair I felt seconds ago evaporates. We're going to make it!

We reach the helicopter. More and more werewolves are closing on us, but it doesn't matter. Liam, Stephen, and the injured Leo cut down those closest to the helicopter and stand guard outside, keeping the area clear while the rest of us clamber in.

Shark and Timas bundle into the cockpit. Shark whoops and tries to start the engine. There's no response. He frowns, ducks, looks beneath the control panel. Comes up pale-faced. "They removed . . ." He curses, then stares at Timas with wild hope. "Any way you could . . . ?"

Timas takes his nose out of Pip's backpack long enough to peer down. "No," he says. "This is going nowhere." He continues rummaging through the backpack.

"The boats," Meera gasps. "Werewolves can't swim."

"It would take at least two minutes to lower a boat," Prae says miserably. "We could cut one free and drop it, but we'd still have to climb down the ladders. They'd clamber after us or hurl themselves off the cliff on top of us. We'd never make it."

"I could put a shield in place at the top of the ladder," I pant.

"You'd need a bigger shield than that," Timas murmurs. "Didn't you notice the slits in the cliffside walls of the compound when you were studying the maps? They're so the guards can fire at anything attacking from the seaward direction. They can pick us off if we try to descend."

"Could you cover us from gunfire and werewolves all the way to the bottom?" Shark asks.

"I don't know," I groan. "I can try."

"I don't like it," he growls. "We'd be too exposed. Any other suggestions?"

"Can you get us inside the compound again?" Meera asks Prae.

"No. I don't know the security codes."

"Timas?"

"I could figure them out," he says calmly, "but it would take several minutes."

There's a scream. Leo goes down, tackled by a pair of small werewolves. Liam and Stephen fire into them, but it's too late. When they fall away, Leo's eyes are wide and lifeless, a shredded mesh where his throat should be.

"Out of time," Shark sighs. "Let's try for the boats and just hope for —"

"Caves!" I shout, flashing on an image of a map of the island. I grab Prae's right arm. "Are there caves near here?"

"I don't know." She scowls. "I wasn't involved with this project. I haven't —"

"There are a few within reach," Timas cuts in. He looks at me curiously. "What sort of cave are you interested in?"

"One with a single entrance, so we can block it off and seal ourselves in."

"What will that achieve?" Shark frowns.

"If I have a few hours, I can open a window to the Demonata universe."

Shark stares at me, then the boats, then the breached perimeter wall and the hordes of werewolves flooding through. He calculates the odds.

"If we don't make it to the cave, we can break for the sea and jump off one of the cliffs," Timas says thoughtfully.

"So we'd have a plan B." Shark nods. "OK. The cave. Go for it!"

Spilling out of the helicopter, we face the oncoming ranks of werewolves and press stubbornly — suicidally — forward into the thick of them.

Barbaric madness. Blasting our way through the wild, fast, powerful, stinking, howling creatures. Shark, Timas, Liam, Stephen, Spenser, and Prae gather in a tight circle around Meera and me. They stand three on either side, backs pressed in against us. We move like a crab, edging forward awkwardly. The soldiers and Prae shower the werewolves with bullets, but it won't be long before one breaks through, then another, then all.

"This is crazy!" I yell, changing my mind. "We'll never make it. Let's try the boats."

"No," Timas responds. "If we reach the wall, we'll be over the worst. Notice how the flow of werewolves has lessened? Most of the beasts within quick reach of the compound are already here."

"So?" Shark shouts, never taking his eyes off the beasts, firing every few seconds, measuring his bullets carefully, not wasting any.

"I have a plan," Timas says. "It should buy us some time."

"What sort of a plan?" I ask suspiciously.

Timas jiggles Pip's backpack at me. "The sort that goes *boom*!"

One of the larger, incredibly muscular werewolves leaps through the air. Bullets from more than one gun lace his body, but he lands on top of Spenser and yanks him away from us. The werewolf tumbles after the soldier and drops dead a second later. But the damage is done. Spenser's cut off. Before he can rejoin the group, half a dozen wolfen savages are covering him. He dies screaming a woman's name.

We push on, no time to mourn our fallen friend. I'm itching to use magic, but I have to save myself. No point wasting my energy on getting to the cave if I can't open a window to safety once we're there.

We creep closer to the wall, the werewolves dogging our every step, snapping and clawing at us, trying to press through the rain of bullets. I notice that most of the larger beasts are hanging back behind the smaller specimens. They must be some of the enhanced creatures, those who were physically and mentally altered, trained to hunt in packs. They're letting the weaker creatures hurl themselves at us, to tire us, so they can move in when we're more vulnerable.

According to Timas, the Lambs created more than two hundred of these newer, deadlier werewolves. I can't count more than fifty around us. That means the rest must be spread across the island — or waiting for us outside the wall.

I think about sharing this potentially fatal piece of news with the rest of the team, but see no point in freaking them out. If a hundred-plus of the stronger, smarter savages are lying in ambush, we're finished. No point worrying the others. If that's our fate, let their last few minutes be filled with hope instead of dread.

✠ ✠ ✠

✠ We make the wall without any more casualties. Shark and the soldiers look completely drained. But they never slow or waver. True professionals, driving themselves on past the point of exhaustion.

We move into one of the gaps in the wall and pause at a shout from Timas. He, Shark, and Liam train their weapons on the mass of werewolves on the compound side of the wall. Stephen and Prae cover the rear, picking off the stray werewolves who haven't invaded yet or are just arriving.

"Give me a few seconds," Timas says once we've established our precarious position. He slips out of his place, passing Meera his gun.

"I don't know how to use this," she screeches.

"Point it at a target and pull the trigger," Timas says. "I've set it to its simplest mode." He nudges her forward with an elbow, then digs into Pip's backpack and produces several small devices. He hands a few to me.

"Do I just throw them?" I ask.

"I'd rather you simply held them for me," he says, fiddling with those in his own hands. "If they're not lobbed accurately, they might explode in the wrong direction. That would be bad for us."

"Timas!" Shark shouts. "We can't hold much longer. They're crowding in."

"My plan wouldn't work if they didn't," Timas says, then gently tosses one of his devices forward. It lands a yard ahead of us, less than six feet from the rabid wave of werewolves.

"Close your eyes," he purrs, lobbing another bomb after the first, then covering his face with an arm.

The first device explodes as I snap my eyes shut. The second explosion follows almost instantly. Screams replace howls. I chance a look. It's like a bulldozer has plowed through the werewolves ahead of us. Dozens are on the ground, dead or bleeding, whimpering and confused. Those to the sides are barking with anger and fear, backing away from the carnage. Before they can recover their wits, Timas lobs three more devices, one left, one right, one straight ahead.

"These are a bit more destructive than the first two," he warns. "You might want to cover your ears also."

His warning comes just in time. I've only barely jammed my hands over my ears when the devices explode. The vibrations shake my brain around inside my skull. When I look again, the devastation is unbelievable, like a field of dead in a war movie. Those not caught by the blasts are scrambling backwards, yowling with pain, ears and noses bleeding. Werewolves have much sharper senses than humans. This must be sheer agony for those not killed.

Timas turns neatly and takes another device from me. Looking back, I see that the creatures on the other side of the wall have come to an uncertain halt. Several are rubbing at their ears and whining. Nowhere near as disorganized as those who bore the brunt of the explosions, but shaken all the same.

When Timas lobs the bomb at them and it explodes, the surviving werewolves bolt like a pack of panic-stricken dogs.

Timas tips an imaginary hat to them, twirls like a ballerina, grabs another device from me, and throws it at those on the compound side. The werewolves might not be the brightest creatures in the world, but they've seen enough to know that when the tall red-headed guy throws something, it means trouble. Roaring abominably, they break and flee, even the enhanced beasts.

We don't waste time congratulating Timas, just bolt for the freedom of the island beyond the wall, determined to take full advantage of the lull, certain it won't last long. Timas is the only one who doesn't run immediately. He remains behind, setting more devices in the ground between the gap in the wall.

Moments later he catches up with us and retrieves the bombs that I've been holding. His backpack looks pretty flat now, but he doesn't seem worried. He grins at me as he pockets a couple of the explosives. "That was the first practical experience I've had of controlled detonations," he says.

I gape at him. "You'd never used a bomb before?"

"No. I'd read about them, but this was the first chance I had to put my knowledge to the test." He looks back and frowns at the hole in the wall, the cloud of dust in the air, the dismembered bodies of the butchered werewolves. "What do you think? Eight out of ten, or am I being too generous?"

"Shut up, you genius of an idiot," I laugh. "And run!"

We race to the top of a small incline, Timas leading the way. We pause to catch our breath and gather our wits. I can already see a few werewolves sniffing around the gap in the wall. As they creep through, one steps on a landmine and sets it off. The others scatter at top speed.

I feel like cheering, but I don't want to tempt fate. Besides, it won't take them long to try one of the other, unmined gaps. Once they discover a safe way out of the compound, they'll pursue us again, only this time they'll be even more determined to hunt us down, to make us pay.

Timas sets another couple of devices at the top of the little hill, covering them with loose earth, like someone planting seeds.

"What else do you have in there?" Shark asks, nodding at the backpack.

"Not much," Timas sighs. "I have a few mines in my pockets and some grenades in case we run into resistance. As for the rest . . . enough to bring down the cave entrance. There won't be much left over."

"Did anybody else notice the larger breeds?" Prae pants. "At the rear?"

"Yes," I answer softly, but I'm the only one.

"Horwitzer's work," she growls. "They're even deadlier than the others. They hung back where it was safe, waiting for the ideal moment to strike. If there are more of those, or if they catch up with us before we make it to the cave . . ." She shakes her head.

"If Timas is right, there's a couple of hundred of them in total," I tell her.

Prae's face goes ashen.

"None of that," Shark snarls, snapping his scorched fingers in front of her eyes. "We won't have pessimism. By any account we should be dead already. But we're not. Having come through that, we can survive anything. If you disagree, keep it to yourself."

Prae chuckles weakly, then pushes to her feet and looks over the island. I stand and stare too. We can't see anything except grassland, which gives way to bushes and trees. But I can hear the howls of werewolves. They're getting closer.

"Shark," I say nervously.

"I know." He stretches, then groans. "My back's killing me. Never had trouble before. I might have to think about retiring after this one."

We all laugh. It's the free and edgy laughter of people who've come through hell and lived to tell the tale, but have to face the journey at least one more time.

Shark clicks his tongue and everyone rises. Liam and Stephen are covered in blood, filth, and scraps of hairy flesh. Meera hasn't returned Timas's gun, but is cradling it like a baby. Prae's trembling, but holding herself together. Only Timas looks unconcerned, as if we're on a leisurely stroll. The rest of us are beaten and worn.

But we're alive. And that gives me hope. We might make it off this island yet, damn the odds. If we do, it'll rank as one of the greatest escapes ever, up there with Beranabus's finest death-defying shimmies. I almost want to survive just to prove to the magician that he's not the only cat with nine lives.

If he's still alive. Thinking about him reminds me of Juni's taunt, that Dervish, Bec, and Beranabus have been set upon by the Shadow. Are they in an even worse spot than us? Has Beranabus been catapulted into the afterlife ahead of me, along with Bec and my uncle?

Before I can dwell on that grim possibility, Shark barks a command. As we sprint down the opposite side of the incline, all other fears and thoughts are forgotten. Running . . . werewolves . . . the cave. There's no room inside my head for anything else.

CAVEMEN

THE howls intensify as we run, coming from all directions, a cacophony of wolfen roars tightening around us like a net. But we don't spot another werewolf until, cutting our way through a small copse, one leaps from a tree without warning and drags Shark to the ground. The pair roll away from us, and though the soldiers in our group swiftly train their weapons on the beast, I'm sure they're too late. I resign myself to the loss of our leader.

But Shark isn't ready for the grave just yet. Staggering to his feet, he shoulders the howling werewolf away. The others can't shoot because he's in their way, and Shark lost his gun in the attack.

"Down!" Stephen yells, desperate to put a bullet through the werewolf's head.

Shark has other ideas. Jerking a knife from his belt, he leaps on the savage beast and drives the blade into its stomach, chewing on its left ear for extra impact. The werewolf screams and claws at Shark's back, ripping his shirt and much of his flesh to shreds. But Shark jabs at it a second time and a third, and its hands drop away. Moments later he shrugs it off and hobbles free.

"Are you OK?" Meera asks as he rejoins us, casting a worried look at his injuries.

"I've cut myself worse shaving," Shark grunts. He retrieves his rifle and pushes up beside Timas, ignoring the blood pooling around the waistband of his pants.

As we clear the copse, we spot an army of werewolves surging towards us from our far left. The beasts at the front look like they're part of the enhanced breed. We can also hear crashing and snapping sounds in the trees behind us — the pack from the compound has almost caught up.

"There!" Timas shouts, swiveling right. I can't see anything except a lot of rocks jutting out of the ground, but he seems sure of himself. As we hurl ourselves after Timas, I pray desperately that his map-reading skills were as accurate as he led us to believe.

I don't look back as we run, but I hear the werewolves closing in. The creatures who've been chasing us from the compound have merged with those arriving fresh on the scene to create a chorus of howls and screeches that could drown out the sound of a nuclear detonation. I feel hot breath on the back of my neck. I hope it's just my imagination.

Timas reaches a rock, grabs it with his left hand, and pivots, lobbing a bomb over our heads as he swings out of sight. The explosion and screams of the werewolves are music to my ears. But as I come in line with the rock and duck around it, I catch sight of the beasts, no more than several yards behind, and my glee shrivels up like the petals of a flower at the heart of a furnace.

There's no sign of Timas. For a horrified second I think he's been snatched by a werewolf. But then I see his bony arm and narrow fingers jerk out of a hole, beckoning us on.

Shark is next to make it. He dives in, and Timas's arm disappears. The rest of us come abreast of what looks like just a hole in the rock, fewer than three feet high. But as I look closer I see that the floor is lower than the ground out here, so you can stand inside. It's more of a tunnel than an actual cave, but I'm not going to complain about that.

Shark pops up like a jack-in-the-box. He aims over our heads and fires at the werewolves. There's a grunt three or four inches behind my ear and I realize they're even closer than I feared.

Screaming madly, I wrap an arm around Meera's waist and hurl her into the hole, like a basketball player making a slam dunk. She smashes against one of the walls inside the entrance and cries out with pain. But at least she's out of the reach of the werewolves.

Prae ducks in after Meera and scurries forward. I almost collide with Stephen as we both try to push in at the same time. We pause and I flash on a ridiculous image of us standing here, politely muttering, "No, after *you,*" until we're carved up and consumed. But then Stephen slaps my back and I gratefully dive in ahead of him.

Meera and Prae have shuffled deeper into the cave. Timas is hooking up a series of devices to the walls around the entrance. For once he isn't grinning. By his expression, you might even think he was slightly perturbed.

Shark is still standing half out of the cave, roaring as he empties his cartridge into the hordes of werewolves. Stephen falls into the cave backwards, firing as he topples. He takes out a werewolf that was just about to snap Shark's head off.

"Back!" Timas yells.

Shark immediately withdraws. Liam, who was covering the rest of us from outside, dives into the hole after him. But he comes to a stop mid-air, arms outstretched, legs caught. He screams. Shark curses and grabs for Liam's hands. He catches them and tugs hard. Liam screams again.

"Hold on!" Stephen shouts, wriggling forward, firing around Shark and Liam.

Liam jerks forward a few inches. It looks like Shark has him, but then he's wrenched out of the cave. For a brief moment I'm dazzled by sunlight. Then the hole fills with the heads and upper torsos of dozens of werewolves. They snap and lash at each other, fighting to be first in.

Before the werewolves can sort themselves out and slither into the cave, Timas yells, "Everybody down!" I catch sight of him pushing a button on a tiny detonator as I leap for safety. Then there's the mother of all explosions and the roof around the entrance comes crashing down, muting the howls of the werewolves, plunging us into darkness, entombing us beneath the ground.

Nobody says anything for several minutes. We can't — the air's clogged with dust and bits of debris. We crawl away from the rubble in search of cleaner air, heads low, covering our faces with jackets and T-shirts, breathing shallowly. The roof slopes downwards and after a while we have to bend. When that becomes uncomfortable, we sit and wait for the air to clear. I'm exhausted. I could happily fall asleep where I'm sitting.

Shark breaks the silence. He coughs, spits out something, then says, "Who's still alive?"

"Me," Timas answers brightly.

"Me," Prae Athim gasps.

"Me," Stephen says morosely — I think he was good friends with Liam.

"Me," I mutter through the fabric of my T-shirt, not ready to chance the air yet.

"Me," Meera groans, "though I feel like half my ribs are broken. What the hell did you throw me in for, Grubbs?"

"I was trying to save you," I growl.

"I could have saved myself," she snaps.

"Ungrateful cow!"

"Chauvinist pig!"

We laugh at the same time.

"Cute," Shark huffs. "Now somebody tell me they brought a flashlight." Nobody says anything. "Brilliant. So we're stuck here in the —"

Something glows. I tug my T-shirt down and squint at the dim light. It's coming from Timas's gun, from the small control panel I noticed earlier. Humming, Timas makes a few adjustments and the glow increases, just enough to illuminate the area around us. He looks up. His grin is firmly back in place, though it looks a bit eerie in the weak green light.

"Remind me to kiss you when this is over," Shark says, struggling not to smile.

"Me too," Meera adds. "Seriously."

Timas shrugs as if it's no big thing, then raises his rifle so we can see more. We're in a tight, cramped cave (or spacious tunnel, depending on how you look at it). The roof is much lower than it was at the entrance and dips even more farther back. The rocks are jagged and jab into me. The floor is sandy and littered with sharp stones. It's humid and dusty from the explosion. But I'm too grateful to be alive and in a werewolf-free zone to feel anything but utter delight — love, almost — for our surroundings.

"How far back does this run?" Shark asks.

"That information wasn't on the charts," Timas says, then sets his rifle down. "Wait here." He crawls away from us. We wait, breathing softly, nobody needing to be told that air might be precious. Timas is gone for what feels like two minutes . . . three . . . four.

I see him returning before I hear him. He can move in almost perfect silence when he wishes. He returns to his rifle, picks it up, and sets it on his lap. "The news is both positive and negative," he says. "The cave is approximately one hundred feet long, but it doesn't finish with a wall. There's a small gap between roof and floor. Air is blowing through from the other side. So we needn't fear suffocation."

"That sounds good to me," Shark says. "What's the bad news?"

"The floor isn't solid." Timas scrapes a nail through the layers of sand, grit, and small stones beneath us.

"So?" Shark growls.

"This area is riddled with small caves and tunnels. I've no idea how large the opening on the other side of the hole is — it wasn't on any of the maps — but if it's large enough to permit entry, or if it can be enlarged, and the werewolves catch our scent, they'll be able to burrow through."

Shark frowns. "If the hole's small, we could block it."

"Yes," Timas says, "but that won't hold them. As I said, the floor isn't solid. With their claws, it wouldn't take them long to dig through. We could shoot the one in front and use its body to jam the entrance. But the soil here is extremely poor. Others would be able to dig under or around it.

"But, hey," he adds with a shrug. "It might never happen."

"Let's assume it will," Shark sniffs, then peers around for me. "What about that window you promised?"

"I'll get to work on it." I lean against the wall and rotate the creaks out of my neck. I'd kill for Tylenol.

"Do you need us to be silent, get out of your way or anything?" Shark asks.

"No." I close my eyes, reaching down to the magic within me. As the others start discussing the situation, I drown out their voices. There are all sorts of ways to open windows, depending on the mage or magician. Some need to sacrifice a human or even themselves. Most just use spells. A powerful mage can open a window in half a day, no matter where they are, while others need several days.

I've only opened windows twice before, once in the cave

where Beranabus was based before he started searching for the Shadow. The other was in an area within the demon universe. Both times there was plenty of magic to tap into, and I managed to complete the window within a couple of hours. It will be hard and slow this time. I told Shark I could do it in a few hours but it might take me —

Between seven and eight hours, says the voice of the Kah-Gash, startling me.

"Where were you when I needed you?" I growl silently.

It won't be enough time, the Kah-Gash says, ignoring my criticism.

"What do you mean?"

The werewolves will work their way through within the next hour. They have your scent and a few of the smarter creatures are already searching for another way in. They'll find it.

I curse, then ask the Kah-Gash if it can help us.

You can help yourself, it replies with typical vagueness. *First, get out of here. I'll explain the rest when I have to. You must trust me and act quickly when I give the order. There won't be much time.*

"Then why not tell me now?" I grumble, but it's gone silent again.

Sighing, I open my eyes and debate whether I should try to build a window regardless. Beranabus is wary of the Kah-Gash. He's not sure if we can use it or if it might attempt to use us instead. Maybe it's trying to trick me. Perhaps it wants me to die here, so that Juni can harvest my soul and present it to her new master.

As I'm mulling over my decision, I listen to the conversation around me. Prae is outlining her fall from grace, how Antoine Horwitzer outfoxed her.

"I knew about some of the experiments," she says, "but I didn't know he'd taken things this far. I sensed something foul when I found out he was training packs to hunt. That served no curative purpose. I delved deeper, exposed more of the rot, and revealed my misgivings to the board."

"Let me guess," Meera says drily. "They betrayed you?"

"I don't think they were all involved" — Prae scowls — "but most of the members were on Horwitzer's side. Next thing I knew, I was being packaged up and posted here, where I've been stewing for the last month or however long it's been."

"Dervish thought the Lambs were rotten at the core," Meera says bitterly. "That's why he had so little to do with them. But he never guessed they might be in league with the Demonata."

"I knew nothing about that," Prae protests. "Dervish never told me anything about demons, even though I pleaded with him to share his information. If he'd been more forthcoming, perhaps —"

"Don't you dare," Meera growls. "This isn't Dervish's fault. And even if you weren't dancing to Antoine's tune, you certainly played along when it suited. You already confessed to knowing about some of the experiments. I bet you knew about the breeding program, right?"

"Not that they'd been bred in vast numbers or to such an altered state," Prae says quietly.

"But you knew the basics. You approved the general aims of the project. Yes?"

"We needed more specimens," Prae sighs. "Where else could we get them?"

"I bet you didn't let your daughter breed," Meera sneers.

Prae stiffens. "What do you know about Perula?"

"Nothing," Meera says. "But she wasn't one of those picked to be experimented on, was she? You wouldn't do that to your own daughter. It wasn't a case of progress at any price. You spared your own."

Prae looks at Meera miserably and, to my surprise, I feel sorry for the deposed Lamb. I sense guilt stirring within her. Prae believed she was following the path of righteous experimentation. Now she's seen the flipside. Antoine Horwitzer could never have made his move if Prae hadn't done so much of the groundwork. She's responsible for a lot of this, and awareness of that must hurt like hell.

But that doesn't matter. If the werewolves dig through, the innocent will perish just as gruesomely as the guilty. I have to decide whether I can trust the voice of the Kah-Gash. Since I don't have any real alternative, I choose to heed its advice.

"I can't build a window."

The others look at me, startled.

"What's wrong?" Meera gasps. "Has Juni cast a spell against you?"

"No. There isn't time. The werewolves will find the other entrance. They'll be on us inside an hour."

"That's an interesting prediction," Timas says. "What are you basing it on?"

"Magic." I lock gazes with Shark. "We have an hour. I can't open a window that quickly."

"Try," he snarls.

I shake my head. "I'd just waste my power. We need to find another way."

"There isn't any," he says icily. "You were our only hope once we chose this cave over the other options."

"I don't think many werewolves are going to gather at the other side," I tell him. "Only the smartest ones have thought of looking for another entrance. I doubt if they'll share their find with the rest — they'll want us for themselves. If we can get through those few . . ."

"What?" Shark laughs cruelly. "Fly out of here? Find another cave?"

"There isn't one nearby," Timas says.

"See?" Shark spits.

"But we're close to water," Timas adds. "Maybe a three- or four-minute run. The cliff is much lower there than around the compound. We could jump and probably survive the fall. From this point we're out of sight of those in the compound, so we could swim to another island."

"Where I could open a window!" I cry, excited.

"I don't like it," Shark says stubbornly. "We should stay here and stick to our original plan. You can't know for sure that they'll find . . ."

A vibrating howl stops him. It drifts to us from the

narrowest point of the cave. Seconds later we hear the echoes of soft scrabbling sounds, distant, but not distant enough for comfort.

"An hour," I repeat glumly.

Shark sighs and raises a weary eyebrow at Timas. "You held back some of the explosives?"

"A few, for an emergency," Timas confirms.

"Good." Shark cracks his knuckles. "I think we're going to need them."

THE FINAL PUSH

WE wait for them to dig through to us. It's horrible, sitting here helplessly, the sounds of the tunneling werewolves growing louder, coming closer. We can hear them snuffling and whining softly, hungrily. The only positive thing is that there don't seem to be many of them. It looks like I was right about the smarter few opting to keep us for themselves.

The downside is that the smarter beasts are also the stronger, faster, deadlier creatures. But we'll happily take the fiercer few over the weaker masses. Shark did an ammunition tally earlier. They're all down to one rifle each, none of them full, no spare clips. They have handguns that won't last long. They won't be able to keep the werewolves back with sustained fire like before. If we have more than a few dozen beasts to deal with between here and the sea, we'll run dry in no time and it'll be hand-to-hand combat after that.

While we're waiting, the glow from Timas's gun fades, then dies, leaving us in complete darkness. Luckily Timas has already set his explosives, so it doesn't affect our plans, just our nerves.

The werewolf within me is excited by the closeness of its twisted kin. It wants to dig from this side of the hole and link up with its soulmates. I'm tempted, in a sick way, to unleash it and let it loose on Shark, Meera, and the others. It's a bit like the feeling I get when I'm standing on a cliff or high building, looking down at a suicidal drop. I start thinking about what would happen if I stepped off, the rush of the fall, the shattering collision, the quiet emptiness of death. Part of me wants to experience the thrill of complete surrender. . . .

But I've always ignored that niggling voice and I ignore it now. Hold tight. Stay focused. Wait.

✠ We can smell them now and hear their labored panting. We've moved down the cave, as close to the lowest point as we can crawl. I thought it would have made more sense to stay back from the blast, but Timas insists he knows what he's doing. "Time is of the essence," he says. "We have to risk getting singed."

The werewolves sound like they're no more than a few feet away. Maybe the first one is already sticking its head through, sliding into our cave. Impossible to tell in the darkness. I want Timas to detonate the bombs immediately, before it's too late, but he only hums and whistles, waiting . . . waiting. . . .

Finally, when I think my nerves are going to snap, Timas whispers, "Shut your eyes, cover your ears, and keep your fingers crossed." A second or two later the rocks explode outwards. I'm struck by a few chips and stony splinters, but they're only scratches. Light floods the cave. I open my eyes, but can't see very far through the dust cloud.

"Go!" Timas coughs, and we crawl on our knees until we can stand and run crouched over.

Scraps of flesh, bones, guts, and hair line the floor. Blood's everywhere, making it slippery underfoot. My stomach rumbles. It's been a long time since breakfast. The wolfen part of me would happily tuck in and make short work of the offal.

We stumble out of the tunnel, Stephen and Shark in the lead, Meera and me in the middle, Timas and Prae bringing up the rear. The sunlight is glorious after the darkness of the cave, but there's no time to lap it up. A couple of werewolves are staggering around, bloodstained, shaking their heads, dazed. No sign of any others. We've come through on the far side of the rocky outcrop, out of sight of the multitudes.

"Come on," Shark hisses. "Let's —"

A growling sound from my left. I whirl and catch sight of a werewolf leaping through the air. It was hiding behind a rock. Three others emerge from behind similarly sized rocks. The cunning beasts have set an ambush!

The first werewolf lands on Shark and knocks away his rifle. Shark snarls as the werewolf growls. He grabs its head and jerks it left then right, trying to snap the beast's neck before it chews his face off.

Stephen makes the crucial mistake of aiming at the

werewolf attacking Shark instead of the other three behind it. Two of them tackle him as he squeezes off his first shot. He yelps, then he's gone, covered by the werewolves, their claws and fangs glinting in the sunlight as they tear into him. He doesn't even have time to scream.

The final werewolf bounds towards Meera, Prae, and me. Meera raises her rifle and the beast stops and glares at us — it clearly knows what a gun is, the damage it can cause. It looks around. Stephen's bullet struck the first werewolf just above its heart, wounding but not killing. It's still struggling with Shark and has driven him back into the tunnel. He's managed to free his knife and is slicing at the beast's throat.

The werewolf who was coming after us chooses the easier option. It changes direction and dives after Shark, driving him farther back. Meera fires at it. Misses. Starts after it, to help Shark.

"Get the hell out of here!" Shark bellows, smashing the first werewolf's face with an elbow, ducking to grab the second by its waist. He whirls it around and hurls it away. "Go!" he screams at us furiously as the werewolf regains its feet and leaps at him again.

"Come on," Timas says, tapping my shoulder.

"But —" Meera and I start to protest at the same time.

"Stay and die," Timas says calmly, "or run and live. Your choice." He sets off, Prae Athim just behind him.

Two of the werewolves are still snacking on Stephen. The other two are forcing Shark farther back. There are no more in sight, apart from the befuddled few we first spotted. But it's surely a matter of seconds rather than minutes before others come running to investigate the explosion and howls.

I find myself moving before I consciously make the decision, my feet one step ahead of my brain. Shark's our leader. He gave us an order to run. We'd be fools if we ignored him, and Shark never tolerated fools gladly.

My last glimpse of the burly ex-soldier is of him wrestling with one werewolf, while keeping the other at bay with his knife, backing up into the shadows of the tunnel, conceding ground reluctantly, stubbornly. Then the dust from the explosion enfolds and obscures him and the werewolves, swallowing them whole.

With a cry of hate and fear, I turn, grab Meera, and flee after Timas and Prae. It seems hopeless without Shark. I was sure he'd be the last of us to fall. Without him all is surely lost. But he went down fighting and the rest of us owe it to him to give it our best shot. If we fail, we should at least die valiantly — like Shark.

The scent of the sea thickens in my nostrils as we run, drawing me towards it. There are howls behind us. The werewolves have found our trail again. But we've worked up a solid lead. We have half a chance.

"This is it," Timas pants as we struggle up a steep rise. "When we get to the top . . . it's two hundred feet. . . to the edge . . . give or take a few . . . yards." He sneaks a quick look back. His brow creases and his large eyes narrow. "We won't make it. They'll catch us."

"We have to . . . try," I cry, lungs bursting, legs aching.

"Someone has to lie down . . . covering fire," he says. "I'll stop at the . . . top and make my last . . . stand."

"No!" Meera shouts. "We've lost too many already."

"We'll all die if I don't," Timas says simply.

"I'll do it," Prae gasps. She's lagging a few paces behind the rest of us. "I'm the slowest. Besides, they're *my* werewolves."

"I'm a better shot," Timas says. "This is my job. It makes more sense . . . for me . . . to stay."

"What the hell," Prae wheezes. "Let's both do it . . . and die together."

"As you wish." We're almost at the top. Timas slaps my back. "One last push and . . . you're there. Don't slow or look back. Run, jump, swim. Meera . . ." She looks around. "I'm sorry I won't . . . be able to claim . . . that kiss you promised."

"Don't worry," Meera says. "I lied. I wouldn't have kissed you anyway." The tall man's face drops and Meera groans. "I'm joking!"

Timas's smile lights up his face again. With a cheerful wave he stops, turns, swings his rifle around, and opens fire. Glancing over my shoulder, I see Prae halt, drop to her knees, take aim. The werewolves are damn close, dozens of them, the larger, enhanced members to the front, leading the pack.

I mount the crest of the rise after Meera. The clifftop lies enticingly ahead of us, the two hundred feet away that Timas calculated. My heart leaps in my chest. I catch up with

Meera. We're going to make it! I don't care if we perish when we dive, if the tide's out, or if we're driven under by vicious currents. At least we won't die here on this cursed, savage island of . . .

Werewolves. Streaming towards the edge of the cliff from our left and right. They've split into two groups and flanked us. The smarter beasts must have guessed our plan. Rather than waste themselves on Timas and Prae, they branched around. As we watch in horror, they dart ahead of us and form a barrier across the top of the cliff, two or three bodies deep. Some remain to the sides, to ensure we don't veer off.

We come to a stop. Meera points her gun at the creatures ahead of us, then does a quick headcount and lets it drop. She looks at me and shrugs. We share a bitter smile. I'd like to hug her, but I haven't the energy. With incredible weariness we half-crouch and cross our arms on our knees. We're panting like thirsty dogs, surrounded, trapped, waiting for the werewolves to close in and brutally finish us off.

THE BEAST WITHIN

✠ ✠ ✠

ONE of the werewolves howls commandingly. A couple to his left and right return the cry, along with a few on the flanks and behind us. But when those howls die away, there's silence, which is more unsettling than the noise. I've gotten used to the violent baying of these beasts. Silence seems creepier.

Scrabbling noises behind us. I cock my head and look back. Timas and Prae scramble over the rise, guns raised but not firing. They stop when they spot us and the ranks of werewolves beyond. Prae looks confused. She turns slowly in a circle, studying the ring of twisted creatures, then shuffles towards us. Timas advances beside her, walking backwards, rifle still aimed. Werewolves from the other side follow them as far as the top of the incline, then stop at a howl from the one near the cliff.

"This is amazing," Prae says, joining Meera and me. "They have a group leader. Even those that haven't been modified are obedient. There are other dominant members too." She points out a few of the larger werewolves. She's excited by the discovery, momentarily forgetting her fear. "I never would have believed it if I hadn't seen it. I doubt even Antoine knows about this. His experiments succeeded far beyond his aims. They've become a true pack." There are tears of happiness in her eyes.

"What happens if we kill the leader?" I ask. "Will the rest split?"

"Of course not," she snorts. "One of the other dominant members would replace him. Or her — maybe the females are superior." She sighs. "I wish I had time to conduct a thorough study."

At a howl from the group leader — one of the largest werewolves, with dark grey hair — the pack starts to close around us. A couple of the smaller werewolves dart forward, but are immediately dragged to the ground and beaten or killed by the dominant members. The rest obediently hold the line.

"We'll hit those at the center and try to squeeze through," Timas says. He still hasn't turned. "Concentrated fire. If we can make them part a few yards, we stand a chance."

"I'm game," Meera says, straightening and picking up her discarded weapon.

"It's hopeless," Prae mutters, but aims her gun too.

Tell them to stop, the Kah-Gash says abruptly.

"Stop!" I gasp. As they look at me questioningly, I hold up a hand for silence and concentrate on my mysterious inner voice.

If they fire now, there will be chaos and you'll all die.

These beasts have become an organized pack. You must use that against them.

"How?" I ask aloud.

Fight them on their own terms.

"I don't know what you mean."

The voice sighs contemptuously. *Do I have to do* everything *for you?* Before I can answer, it says curtly, *Unleash the wolf.*

"Which one?" I frown.

The one inside you, fool!

"I don't —"

We haven't time to argue. I said you'd need to obey me without question. They're closing in. Unleash the wolf. Give it free reign. Trust me.

I hesitate. The werewolf within my skin is something I fear completely. I've gone to great efforts to keep it imprisoned. In my nightmares it has often burst free and caused havoc, killing all around me. I'm determined not to let those dark dreams become reality. The Kah-Gash understands that. It helped me push the werewolf down deep when I didn't know how to do it myself. So why is it telling me to release the beast now? Is this part of the Shadow's plan? Will I play into the hands of the Demonata if I —

Last chance, the Kah-Gash warns as the werewolves creep to within twenty or twenty-five feet of us.

Cursing silently, I reach inside with magic and tear at all the barriers that I've put in place over the last year, ripping them to shreds, pulling down the wall of safeguards that has protected me from my more beastly, bloodthirsty half. The wolf at my core is startled, suspecting a trap. Then, as I encourage it forward, it realizes this is real and leaps to the surface, howling with delight.

My temperature shoots up, my skin tightens, my bones seem to crack, snapping away from each other, thrusting upwards and outwards.

I fall to the ground, crying out with pain. Vaguely aware of Meera shouting, trying to help, and Timas roaring, asking for orders to fire. I shake my head. My eyes are hardening. There's blood in my mouth. I raise a trembling hand and stare at it. The nails lengthen while I watch, fingers curling inward, hairs sprouting from my knuckles. Then my sight flickers and blurs.

My gums split, my teeth grow, my lips extend. I cough, lungs altering, heart pounding faster than it ever did before. Muscles rip and strain, then knot again. White noise fills my ears, threatens to deafen me, then fades, leaving me with a better sense of hearing than ever.

"He's turning into one of them!" Timas cries, open panic in his voice. I sense him leveling his gun at me.

"No!" Meera shouts, grabbing the barrel of his rifle, jerking it sideways.

Sight returns. Colors are different, not as keenly defined, but my field of vision has expanded and I can see more sharply, as if viewing the world through a magnifying glass. I spot Timas and Meera struggling. Prae Athim is gaping at me. The werewolves have stopped and are staring. Some paw the ground, eager to sink their fangs into us, but held in place out of fear of the dominant pack.

Something howls, a cry of jubilation, triumph, and violence. As the muscles in my throat constrict, I realize the howling comes from *me.* As that understanding sinks in, I get to my feet, arms flexing, and gaze down at my new body.

My clothes are ripped and falling off my limbs. I'm naked, but I'm not bothered. What need have animals of clothes?

I howl again with savage exultation. Then I look for the group leader. Finding him, I chuckle throatily and step forward. With a challenging grunt, I beckon him on.

The werewolf snarls. I can smell his uncertainty. He's not sure if I'm human or wolfen. I howl again, clearing matters up. His eyes narrow and, with a howl of his own, he charges. He's huge, arms like trunks, but only slightly bigger than me. I plant my feet, twist, and drive my shoulder into the werewolf's chest.

He's knocked to the floor. Around him, the creatures wail and screech. As he rises, furious, I kick him hard in the side of his head. He falls again. I'm on him before he can rise a second time. Setting my teeth on his throat, I bite. Blood fills my mouth and I drink greedily. This is what the werewolf within me has been waiting for all its life. I could squat here and sup until the sun sets.

But the other dominant werewolves have different ideas. Seeing its chance for glory, one darts forward and latches on to my arm. Sinks its fangs deep into my flesh. I break free of the dead werewolf with a muffled cry of pain, then wrench my arm away and head-butt the challenger. Its skull cracks and it drops.

Another attacks, gibbering madly. I grab it by its crotch and throat, lift it up, hold it over my head, then toss it into the pack. Those it lands on go wild and tear it to pieces.

A fourth werewolf steps forward, the largest yet, with the widest shoulders and longest fangs. A female. She looks edgy. If she was a true leader, she would have led from the beginning. I think she's the strongest creature on the island, but she lacks courage. She's only challenging me now because she thinks she has to, that I'll work my way through the dominant members of the pack, one by one, to ensure complete command.

I leap at the werewolf. She lashes out. I let her fist connect with the side of my head, then laugh. I throw a few punches, gnarled hands flying faster than they did when I was human. The challenger stumbles away from me, dazed. I grab her head, jerk it back, fasten my teeth on her throat [illegible] then growl

The werewolf whimpers. I growl again and the whimpering stops. I release her and shove her away — alive. The beast stands, head lowered, subjugated. I glare at the others in the dominant pack, then sweep my gaze over those they command. I roar a question, but not a single one answers.

Returning to the body of the original leader, I lower my head and chew at his throat, leaving myself open to attack. When the werewolves hold their ground, I know there will be no more challenges. Standing again, I look around victoriously, taking it all in . . . the cowed werewolves, those I've killed, the shocked faces of the three humans. I fill with a sense of power and joy. Raising my head to the sky, I howl long and loud, and all around me the werewolves howl back in obedient, respectful response.

They're *my* pack now.

THE TURNED WORM

✠ ✠ ✠

"GRUBBS?" one of the women gasps, eyes filled with horror. "Is that you?"

I crook my neck and stare at her. There's no Grubbs here. Werewolves don't need names. Tags like that are a human weakness. I think about killing her for daring to address me that way.

"Grubbs?" she says again, taking a hesitant step towards me.

A werewolf howls, warning her off. I roar at it angrily — I can protect myself. It lowers its head and whines. I fix my eyes on the woman. My stomach rumbles. The blood of the previous leader is like honey on my lips. But how much sweeter would the blood of a soft human be?

"Meera!" the other woman snaps. "Don't get too close. He might —"

"Grubbs won't hurt me," the one called Meera says confidently.

I snarl at her arrogance and raise a claw to rip off her face. No one has the right to make decisions for me. This woman's made her last mistake. If I let her get away with it, the others will think they have leeway too. I have to kill her, for the good of the pack, to maintain order.

"Don't be silly," Meera says, smiling weakly at my upraised hand. "You won't hurt me. What would Dervish say if you did? You remember Dervish, don't you?"

I growl uncertainly, hand held above me like a hammer. *Dervish.* The one who guarded me when I needed guarding. Even the wildest beasts have respect for those who rear them. But Dervish isn't here. He's in trouble. He needs help. He's . . .

"Put down your guns," Meera says, dropping hers and crossing her arms.

"Are you sure about this?" the tall man asks.

"What have we got to lose?"

He shrugs and carefully lays down his weapon. The other woman gulps, but follows suit. All three stand shivering, unarmed, at my mercy. I feel the eyes of the pack on me. They have the scent of humans in their nostrils. Their mouths are wet with lust, as is mine. If I deny them their feed, my hold over them will crumble. A leader must do what's right. Part of me wants to spare this trio, but mercy is a luxury I can't afford. It's time to block out the memories of my human past and . . .

Don't be an idiot, a voice says. My eyes flick around with fury, looking for the one who dares speak to me in such a manner. But then I realize the voice is coming from within.

You're a mix of human and werewolf, cemented by magic. You can make new rules.

"But they're hungry," I reply silently. "I am too. We have to eat."

There's plenty of food elsewhere, the voice says slyly, and sends an image of the compound flashing through my brain.

I grin wolfishly, then howl at the pack. They look dubious, so I howl again, fiercer than before, promising them the world, knowing they'll turn on me if I fail to deliver. This time they roar excitedly in response. Those at the rear set off for the compound. Seconds later almost every werewolf on the cliff is streaking inland, eager to be among the first to the feast. Only several of the more advanced beasts hold their place at a commanding cry from me. These, the largest and smartest, will be my personal retinue. They'll travel with me, to dispense my orders. In return, I'll see that they enjoy the lion's share of the spoils.

I face the confused humans and growl softly, trying to communicate. Their expressions are blank — they can't understand. Frowning, I remould the cords of my throat, allowing my face to melt back to something more like its original shape. My teeth retract and my lips soften. I have total control over this body. I realize now that I always did. I could have manipulated myself this way since birth if I hadn't been so afraid of what I might turn into. I'm more than flesh and bone. I'm a spirit, a force, a power. I'm not shackled to any single form.

"Grubbs?" Meera says, searching my eyes for traces of humanity.

"You came *this* close to being eaten," I mumble, eyeing her darkly.

Meera's face fills with relief. "You're *you*!" she cries, throwing her arms around my broader, taller, twisted, hairier body.

"What happened?" Prae asks, studying me with a mix of fascination and horror. "Did the werewolf explode within you?"

"I unleashed it," I explain shortly.

"Are you human or werewolf ?" Timas inquires politely.

"Both." I take a step back from Meera. Her eyes flicker down to my lower body and she raises an eyebrow. I don't blush — werewolves know no shame — but I pick up my discarded pants and tie them around my waist. "We don't have much time," I mutter. "We have to move fast."

"I take it we're not jumping off the cliff now," Meera comments wryly.

"No." I focus on Timas. "Can you get us back into the compound?"

"Yes," he says. "It will take a while, but —"

"Work quickly," I snap. "We're hungry." As the others stare at me, I turn from the sea and break into a trot, eager to feed.

I feel more alive than ever. I'm sure I look awful, no better than any of the mutated werewolves I now command. But I don't care. Looks have never mattered to me less. After all the stress of recent years, the struggle between human, wolf, and Kah-Gash, I've finally found a happy balance. This is who I'm meant to be, not man, werewolf, or magician — but *this.* A mix of all three, uniquely disfigured and warped. For the first time in my life I feel complete.

Meera, Timas, and Prae are afraid of me, and rightly so. If I turned on them, as I'm tempted to, they wouldn't stand a chance. But I choose not to attack. These are my allies, and while I don't feel like I need them anymore — except Timas, to get into the compound — I honor our friendship. Besides, as the Kah-Gash pointed out, there are lots of others I can kill.

The humans struggle to keep up, but I don't make allowances. If they fall behind, they'll have to fend for themselves. I control the werewolves, but I know instinctively that my hold over them is fragile. If I don't maintain complete dominance, I'll lose them.

I can't wait to get my teeth on Juni Swan's throat. Revenge is what I'm focused on. I barely spare a thought for Dervish and the danger he might be in. All I care about is killing the she-fiend who betrayed us. When I've ripped her flesh from her bones and wallowed in her blood . . . then I can turn to other matters. Maybe. Unless I decide to stay here and become ruler of Wolf Island.

The compound. Timas is hard at work on a security access screen. I smell the fear of the soldiers inside. They know we're out here. Several of their finest technicians are united against Timas, playing cat-and-mouse games with him as if locking horns over a chess board. But he's stripping away their defenses, one by one. He's better than they are. It's just a matter of time before he outfoxes them.

By concentrating on my senses of smell and hearing, I

follow the movements of those nearest us. They're lining the tight corridors, checking weapons, preparing to blast wildly at anything that comes through. They're frustrated. If the designers had built slots into these walls, as they did in those at the sides, they could have mowed us down. But an assault like this was never taken into account. The outer wall was meant to hold. The plan, if it fell, was to block off all other entrances to the compound, then escape by boats stored at the rear of the complex. After all, there was no way brainless werewolves could short-circuit the security systems.

The soldiers could flee before we invade, and make a break for freedom. But they've been ordered to stand and fight. Juni doesn't care about losses. It will probably amuse her to watch them die.

She's still there. She has a distinctive, rotting stench. She's waiting for us deep within the compound. I don't know why. Perhaps she thinks she can get the better of me. She's a fool if she does.

A couple of werewolves howl and others take up the cry. They're growing impatient. They aren't ready for mutiny yet, but they're not far from it. Bending close to Timas, I growl, "A few more minutes. Then things get nasty."

"You can't rush a job like this," Timas replies calmly. "I'm going as fast as I can."

"Go faster," I snarl. "When they turn, I won't be able to hold them. I'll be the first they attack, but you won't be far behind."

"Then we'd better hope time is on our side," Timas chuckles, never looking up.

"Leave him alone," Meera snaps. "You're distracting him."

"No, he isn't," Timas says. "I can multitask."

"Do you think they know we're here?" Prae asks, pressing an ear to the wall.

I frown at such a ludicrous question, then remember that she doesn't have the same sharp senses I do. "They know," I tell her. "They're waiting for us."

"Our forces will be cut down," she says quietly, studying the werewolves. "It will be a massacre."

"Many will die," I agree, "but not all. We'll overwhelm them."

"But at such a cost . . . ," Prae sighs. "Is it worth it? Maybe we should just take the boats and get out of here."

"They'd call in fresh troops," Meera says. "They'd fire on the werewolves from the air and wipe them out — they couldn't afford to leave them alive now that we know about Wolf Island. At least this way the beasts have a fair chance."

"I hate this," Prae mutters. "It was never meant to end in a bloodbath. I wanted to save lives, not be responsible for wholesale slaughter."

"Then you shouldn't have become a Lamb," Meera says.

Before Prae can respond, Timas whistles softly. "No more time for bickering. The gates of hell are about to open for business."

He presses a button. Panels slide apart. Werewolves howl and surge forward. A mass of guns discharge at the same time and the air turns red with blood.

THE SHAPE OF THINGS TO COME

✠ ✠ ✠

DOZENS are slaughtered within seconds, torn to ragged, fleshy shreds by the frenzied fire of Juni Swan's soldiers. But the stench of blood only drives the rest of us wilder. We push on without pause, leaping over the jerking bodies of the dead and dying, ignoring the peril, the bullets, the fallen. Not a single beast turns and runs.

I'm among the pack, unable to restrain myself, risking all just to be one of the first to claim a human heart. It's crazy. I should hold back and let them do my dirty work. But for a few mad moments I lose control. I press forward with the others, howling and bellowing, as much of a target as any other werewolf.

Then we're on the terrified soldiers, hacking at them, tearing guns from their hands, chowing down on their sweet, soft flesh and oh-so-chewable bones. Human screams are added to the cacophony of gunfire and howls. The line disintegrates beneath us. I'm past it before I know what's happening, staring at an empty corridor. I have to stop, swivel, and dive back into the fray to claim my victims and be part of the barbaric, bloody feast.

I don't know how much time passes. It could be seconds or minutes. All I'm aware of is the killing and feasting. My world becomes an endless pool of thick, salty blood, springy flesh, brittle bones, juicy inner organs. I butcher heartlessly, wolfishly. I don't know how many. Bodies are tossed around and pulled apart like chicken wings at a party.

When the bloodlust finally passes — when I've had my fill — my senses return. I spit out a mouthful of soggy flesh. I'm drenched in blood, my ears and head ringing with noise. I stare at my red, twisted hands and wait to feel disgust and shame. But nothing hits me. I'm neither appalled nor shocked. In this new form I have no delusions. I'm a killer. Whether a killer of demons, werewolves, or humans . . . no matter. I've butchered with magic in the Demonata universe. Now I've murdered with my hands and teeth here. I feel no more for the people I've slaughtered than the demons I fried. To a beast like me, there's no real difference.

I look around for Meera, Timas, and Prae. I find them standing in a doorway, transfixed, faces pale, eyes awash with horror. Even the usually unflappable Timas Brauss looks disturbed. I sneer at their expressions, wipe a hand across my lips, then lick them clean.

"Sorry I didn't offer you anything to eat," I chuckle hoarsely.

"Grubbs . . . you . . . this . . ." Meera can't find words to express what she feels.

"I did what I had to," I grunt. "It was a fair fight."

"But you enjoyed it!" Meera gasps. "You laughed as you killed. The way you drank . . ."

"I was thirsty," I shrug.

Before Meera can say anything else, I call my private retinue of advanced werewolves to my side. Not all of the chosen come — some are dead. But most assemble, grinning ghoulishly, blood dripping from their chins.

"Let's go and find Juni," I tell them, and over the mounds of dead bodies we climb.

✠ Not all of the soldiers perished at the perimeter. Some dropped back when they realized their cause was lost. They're fleeing through the compound, pursued by ravenous werewolves. I don't know where they think they can hide. It's over. They'll be tracked down and slit from groin to skull. Running only adds sport to the slaughter.

It's hard not to give in to temptation and hunt with the pack. Juni's just one person (or whatever the hell it is that she's become). There are so many others to chase and murder. I have to focus to keep my feral nature in check. I tell myself Juni will be worth it, that the joy of killing her will be greater than a dozen human deaths. But I'm not convinced. I think I might be happier if I surrendered to my desires and ran wild. I'd like to butcher freely while the butchering's good.

I'm aware of Meera, Timas, and Prae arming themselves,

picking guns from the corpses. I don't bother with weapons. I relied on magic and my wits before. Now I have something even better — claws and fangs.

Some of the werewolves sniff longingly at the humans, but the members of my personal guard warn them off with soft growls. Give it a few days and they might not be so obedient. But there's plenty for all to eat now, so they're willing to let these three snack-boxes on legs pass unmolested.

We press farther into the building. The stench of Juni's sickly sweet sweat fills my nostrils. I hope she's sweating with fear, that she's trapped, nowhere to run, dreading our confrontation. If she's not afraid now, I'll show her fear before I kill her. I don't want her to die without knowing what it's like to tremble in the clutches of one more twisted and vicious than yourself.

As I'm closing on her location, I feel a sweep of something like air gushing through the compound. It's warm and tingling. It seeps into my pores, filling me with power.

Magic.

I should be grateful for the extra strength, but I'm not. The wash of magic through the building can mean only one thing — a window has been opened. I'm not afraid of what might come through — I'd fight any number of demons — but I don't want Juni skipping ahead of me to safety in the foul universe she's chosen to call home.

"Quick!" I roar, darting ahead of the others, shouldering a door aside, rushing down a corridor, homing in on the scent of Juni Swan.

"Grubbs!" shouts Meera. "Wait. Don't go in there alone."

But nothing can stop me. A couple of seconds later, wild at the thought that I might miss my chance for revenge, I break through another doorway and into the room where we discovered Prae Athim bound and gagged.

The window hovers near the back of the room, a jagged red panel of light. I dart towards it, meaning to follow Juni, even though I know it's suicide. Then a bolt of energy knocks me sideways. Searing pain eats into my flesh, forcing a scream from my lips.

I stagger and realize I've been tricked. Juni's still here. She was standing to the left of the door. Easy to spot if I'd been paying attention, but I lost my wits for a few vital seconds. Now she has the upper hand.

As I lurch towards her, she mutters a spell and the floor at my feet explodes. Splinters shoot into my stomach, chest and face. I instinctively jerk my head back.

Roaring, I raise a hand to protect my eyes. Ignoring the stinging pain of the splinters buried in my flesh, I set my sights on the pustulant, bloodstained, flesh-dripping Juni Swan. She's smiling insanely. Beyond her, in the doorway, I see Meera and the others, separated from us by an invisible barrier. The werewolves of my retinue are digging at the barrier with their claws, but it will take more than brute force to penetrate Juni's magic shield.

"Did you think I'd leave without saying goodbye?" Juni giggles.

"I'll kill you!" I roar. "I'll rip your head from your neck and —"

"Please don't finish," Juni interrupts. "I detest vulgarity."

She waves a hand at me and the splinters expand and burrow deeper into my skin. I gasp and collapse to my knees. Another couple of seconds and they'll pierce my heart and brain.

If you'll allow me some leeway . . . the voice of the Kah-Gash murmurs. The splinters shoot out of my body and rain down on Juni. That catches her by surprise. With a shriek, she covers her eyes, protecting them as I did. For a moment she's defenseless.

Using the newly developed muscles in my legs, I spring across the room and bowl Juni over. I slam her to the floor and drive a claw into the putrid, oozing flesh of her stomach. She moans, eyes shooting wide, baring her teeth, trembling with agony. I make a fist, grab some of her inner organs and jerk hard. My hand shlups out, trailing guts. Blood splatters the floor. I gurgle with delight.

Juni screams, then covers the hole in her stomach with a hand. Magic flares and the flesh around the hole heals. I don't care. While she's repairing herself, I latch on to her head, jam my fangs into the bone behind her right ear, and start chewing my way through to her brain.

Juni's fresh screams fill me with delight. I almost pull away to enjoy her expression. But I know how dangerous she is. I can't give her any freedom. Best to chew quickly and disable her.

Heat flares in my fangs. I try desperately to bite down. I'm almost through the hard covering of the skull. So close to her brain. But the heat's too much to bear. With a cry of pain and rage, I break free.

Juni's at my throat with incredible speed. Newly grown fingernails dig into the flesh beneath my chin, while the fingers of her other hand tighten around my neck. I sense the fingers stretching, looping, meeting at the back, and melting into each other, tightening into a noose. I try to roar but my vocal cords are squeezed shut.

I slam an elbow into Juni's ribs. Several crack. She grunts, but doesn't release me. She's cackling. Pokes her face up close to mine. Her left eye was punctured, but it grows back as she taunts me.

"Thought you could kill sweet Juni?" she screeches. "Thought a pup like you could overcome a full-grown mistress of dark magic?" Her fingers tighten another notch. "What do you think now, *Grubitsch*?"

I wheeze at her, then manage to get hold of the hand around my throat. Filling my fingers with magic, I sever through the flesh and bones of the noose, then yank myself clear. Panting, I make a fist and smash it into her face. Her nose shatters, splattering me with blood, pus, and slimy snot.

"You look like hell," I snarl.

"You can talk," she sneers, running a scornful eye over my deformed features.

For a moment we grin at each other and get our breath back.

"It's not too late," Juni purrs. "Join us. I sensed you killing those pitiful humans. You've found your true self. Come with me. Put the last vestiges of your useless human morals behind you. With us, you can kill forever. There's a whole world of humans to torment and butcher. You can be a glorious, wolfen god."

"I bet I could have you too," I chuckle darkly.

"Maybe." She smiles. "Lord Loss is my master, but you could be my mate. I can change out of this grotesque form, be any woman you wish. In the new world, anything will be possible."

"There's just one problem," I sigh.

"What?" Juni frowns.

"I hate your guts," I hiss, and spring on her.

I drive my fist towards the hole where Juni's nose used to be. My plan is to jam a few fingers in the gap, widen it, then claw out her brain, scoop by gloopy scoop. But Juni's faster. She ducks, then lashes at my stomach with a leg. I wasn't expecting a bloody kung fu move! I'm sent hurtling backwards and slam hard into the wall. My head cracks and my neck almost snaps.

She's on me before I hit the floor, hands a blur, jabbing incessantly. I try to roar, but all that comes out is a startled croak. I get a glimpse of her throat and lunge for it. Juni shimmies and rams a forearm into my mouth, gagging me. As I choke, she sends what feels like a million volts of magic sizzling through my body. I scream mutedly and go limp. Juni hits me with another burst of energy. Another.

Blood's pumping from my nose, mouth, and ears. Even from my eyes. I'm seeing events through a red mist. I reach deep within myself, looking for the power to strike back, but I'm in disarray.

Forgetting about magic, I lash out at Juni. She laughs, removes the arm from my mouth, and wraps it around me. Squeezes tight, like a boa constrictor.

"Poor Grubbs," she coos, wiping blood from my eyes. "You don't have the hang of magic, do you? You're strong, but experience is everything. My master told me to be wary, but I knew I had the beating of you. When the soldiers and werewolves failed, I decided to finish you off myself."

I spit blood at her. She stops it midair, letting the pearly drops float in front of my eyes. Then she leans forward, extends her tongue and delicately slurps the red pearls from the air, as though tasting an exquisite wine.

"Now it's time to die," she says. Her face is blank. The madness and hatred in her eyes have been replaced by a cold businesslike look.

I struggle feebly. This can't be happening. I'm the pack leader, a magician, part of the Kah-Gash. I've fought and defeated stronger demons than this servant of Lord Loss. I should be dancing on her corpse, not fighting for breath, locked within her suffocating embrace.

"A kiss," Juni hums, pressing her face to mine. "I'll suck your last breath from your body along with your part of the Kah-Gash. I'll take everything and own you completely. You might think it's the end, but your agonies are just beginning. I have the power of death. I'll pluck at the strings of your soul until the end of time, and every strum will draw a thousand screams."

She covers my mouth and inhales, drawing the last of my oxygen from my lungs. I go limp, senses crumpling. It's like she's sucking me down a tunnel into herself. I can't fight. I'm helpless. I'm doomed.

Then, for no apparent reason, she breaks the contact and blinks, staring at me as if stabbed in the back. My heart leaps hopefully. Someone must have found a way past the barrier, snuck up behind her and struck while she was gloating over me. I glance over her shoulder in search of my savior but I can't see anyone.

Juni releases me and takes a step back. Her expression clears and she smiles. Then she laughs, and the laughter strikes me harder than any of her blows. She screams with crazy delight, jumping up and down on the spot, bits of her diseased flesh dropping off like bloated tics.

"Oh Grubbs!" she cries. "You absolute darling. How delicious. How ironic. The savior of the world . . . protector of mankind . . . *Hah!*"

I slump to the floor, take a painful, rasping breath, and stare at Juni. Has she lost herself entirely to madness? Have I been saved by a mental breakdown?

"I just had a vision, darling Grubbs," Juni says, backing up to the window. "I had them all the time when I was Beranabus's assistant. I catch glimpses of the future. That's why he valued my services so highly. I served Lord Loss in the same way when I joined him. That's how we knew the cave in Carcery Vale was going to be reopened, why we acted when we did.

"But this vision was the most vivid ever. You were in it, the star of the show. It was the near future . . . *very* near. You were at your most powerful, tapping into the sort of power that would allow you to crush me like a bug."

Juni sticks a hand through the window. It's pulsing at the edges. It will close soon, but not before she fires off her parting shot.

"I saw the world destroyed," she whispers. "It was blown to pieces. The seas bubbled away, lava erupted, the land split and crumbled. Everyone died, young and old, good and bad. Then a ball of fire burst from the heart of the planet, incinerated the globe and blasted the ashes off into space, before spreading to consume the universe — worlds, suns, galaxies, all.

"You were there," she sobs, crying with happiness. "But you weren't trying to stop it. You made no attempt to save the world. You couldn't . . . you didn't want to . . . because *you* were controlling the mayhem. The Demonata won't destroy your universe, Grubbs Grady — *you* will!"

With that she skips through the window, giggling girlishly. Moaning wildly, I drag myself after her, but before I'm even halfway the window disintegrates, and all I can do is lower my face to the cold, hard, blood-drenched floor and weep.

THE DEVIL'S IN THE DETAILS

✠ ✠ ✠

As magic drains from the air, the barrier blocking the doorway gives way. Meera, Prae, and the werewolves stumble into the room. Timas enters via the hole that Pip blew in one of the side walls earlier. He must have circled around while I was fighting Juni. A dangerous maneuver — he could have been attacked by a rogue werewolf — but he got away with it. Not that it mattered. Juni had blocked that entrance too.

"Grubbs," Meera cries, rushing over. "Are you OK?"

I moan pitifully, reaching for a window that is no longer there, Juni's prediction echoing in my ears. It can't be true. She was mocking me. It's part of some horrible game.

But she had me at her mercy. I was helpless. It would have been a simple matter to finish me off. She spared me because she saw me destroy the world in the future. Nothing else makes sense. I'm more valuable to her alive than dead. I can do what she, Lord Loss, and the Shadow can't.

“You’re wounded,” Meera says, fussing over me. “You have to heal yourself.”

“Leave me alone,” I cry, hammering the floor and cursing.

“The magic’s fading,” Meera hisses. “Use it to heal yourself or you’ll die.”

“Good,” I mutter. Better if I die. I can’t wreck the world if I’m dead.

“Grubbs!” she snaps. “Don’t be an ass. Heal yourself. *Now!*”

I sigh miserably, then focus my power on the bleeding wounds, broken ribs, and ruptured inner organs. It would be for the best if I perished, but I can’t give up on life. I’m not that much of a hero.

“What happened?” Timas asks.

“Didn’t you hear?” I wheeze, working on my chest and upper stomach.

“The sound faded out,” Timas says. “It was like someone turning down the volume on a television set.”

“It was the same for us,” Meera says.

So Juni didn’t want the others to hear her prediction, in case they decided to kill me for the good of mankind. I consider telling them. I’m pretty sure one of them — maybe all three — would put a bullet through my head if they knew of the threat I pose. But that would be another form of suicide, so I hold my tongue and shake my head.

“Just more of the same rubbish,” I grumble. “She said she was sparing me for her master, that Lord Loss wanted to kill me himself.”

"Strange," Timas notes. "She was happy to let the werewolves slaughter you."

"I guess she knew I'd survive. It was all a setup. She never meant for me to die, only the rest of you, so that she could relish my pain."

Timas makes a skeptical humming noise, but says no more. I continue healing myself, Meera watching closely to make sure I don't miss anything. The power's fading fast, but I've dealt with most of the life-threatening injuries. I'll live.

The werewolves — there are five in the room with us — are sniffing the floor by one of the walls. They're growling. I bark at them to be quiet. Listening carefully, I hear scrabbling sounds. Someone's crawling away in a hurry.

"The maps you studied earlier," I say to Timas, rising painfully but standing steady on my feet once I'm up. "Did they show any tunnels or crawlways running off this room?"

"No," Timas says, edging up beside the werewolves.

"Then they weren't as complete as you thought," I sniff.

"You're right," he says, tapping the wall. "There's a hidden panel. I'm sure I can find the opening mechanism if you give me a few —"

I snap at the werewolves. The largest smashes a fist into the metal panel. Again. A third time. It crumples under his fourth blow, snapping loose at the upper and left edges. The werewolf gets a few fingers into the gap and wrenches off the panel, revealing a small passage.

The werewolf who removed the panel darts into the crawlway, but stops at a command from me. Shuffling forward, I stoop and stare into the gloominess. I can't see the person scuttling away from us, but I can smell him. It's a familiar, cultured scent. I smile viciously.

"After me," I say softly, then lower myself to my hands and knees. I edge forward, moving faster than the man ahead of me, steadily catching up, making heavy snarling noises, letting him know I'm coming, savoring the intoxicating smell of his mounting fear.

The crawlway opens out into a large room at the rear of the compound. There are several boats stacked at the sides, but all the hulls have been shattered, holes punched through the shells, making them as seaworthy as sieves. I figure Juni wanted to give her soldiers an extra incentive to stand and fight. She made sure nobody shipped out early.

Antoine Horwitzer is struggling with one of the useless boats, hauling it towards an open section at the far side of the room. I can smell and hear the sea, the crash of the waves, the cries of the gulls. Antoine is sobbing, his jacket tossed to one side, shirt ripped, pants dirty. He must know he can't get anywhere in the boat, but desperation drives him on.

As the others emerge behind me, I raise a hand, holding them in check. Antoine doesn't know we're here. He's totally focused, head bent, straining painfully, using muscles he probably hasn't tested in years. I'm amused by the sight of him dragging the wreck of a boat towards the edge. For a while I forget about Juni Swan and her terrible prophecy, and just enjoy the show.

Finally, when he has about a yard to go, I cough softly.

He freezes. Moans. Gives the boat an especially strong tug. Doesn't look up.

"Antoine," I laugh, stepping towards him.

He looks back, gauging how much farther he has to go. His arms relax and his shoulders slump when he realizes he can't make it. He turns his desolate gaze on me and his eyes widen as he takes in my monstrous form, my blood-soaked body and limbs, my fangs and wolfen face.

"What happened to you?" he gasps.

"Teenage angst," I chuckle. I whistle at the werewolves and they spread out. Meera, Timas, and Prae are directly behind me.

Antoine shrieks when he spots the werewolves. Turns and races for the edge, to leap into the sea below. Drawing from the faint traces of magic in the air, I halt him, exerting an invisible hold over the fallen executive. He struggles wildly, then sees that it's hopeless. Giving up, he faces me.

"I'm going to kill you," I growl, advancing menacingly. "Juni got away, so I'm going to take out all my frustration on you. It will be slow and painful. Suitable payback for the lives you've ruined, the friends of mine you've killed."

"I didn't kill anyone!" he squeals.

"No, your kind never do," I sneer. "You leave it to others. You just set things up and give the orders."

"Please," Antoine sobs, throwing himself to his knees. "Don't do this. It serves no purpose. Put me on trial. Let the proper authorities deal with me. You're not a killer. There's no evil in your soul. Don't —"

"Look at me!" I roar. "Do you think you'll be the first I've killed today? I wasn't a murderer, but you changed me. I'm a monster now. And I'm hungry."

"Meera!" Antoine whines. "Prae! Please, I beg you. You're civilized people. Help me."

"We can't," Prae says coldly. "Even if we wanted to — and personally I have no problem with him gutting you — we couldn't. He's not ours to control. He's one of your *specimens.* You helped create him — now you have to deal with him."

Antoine stares at Prae in disbelief. I draw closer, growling softly in anticipation of the kill. Antoine's eyes harden. "Don't be so hasty, my hairy friend," he murmurs, sounding more like his old self. "There are others to consider."

"Like who?"

"Your uncle," he says smoothly, and I come to an abrupt halt.

Antoine rises, brushing dirt from his shirt and pants. He frowns at his untidy condition, then runs a hand through his hair and shrugs. "I suppose this means an expensive trip to my tailor when I get back."

"You've got five seconds to tell me what you know about Dervish," I snarl.

"Oh, I have more time than that." Antoine grins. "Your uncle's in a perilous situation. There are forces moving against him even as we speak. It will take more than five seconds to —"

"Tell me!" I shout. "Now. Or I'll torture it out of you."

"I'm sure you could," Antoine says slickly, "but how long would it take? I'll hold out as long as I can, just to spite you.

After all, you've already vowed to torment me. I don't know how long I can stand the pain, but minutes are precious. Do you dare waste them?"

I want to throttle him so badly it hurts. But he knows how important Dervish is to me. I don't want to cut a deal with this treacherous viper, but time's against me.

"What do you want?" I growl.

"My life," Antoine replies.

I think about it, then curse. "OK. I won't kill you. Now talk."

"Not so fast," Antoine says. "I want to add a few conditions before I divulge all that I know. Such as a boat without a hole in it, a compass, and map, some —"

"Time's all you have to bargain with!" I snap. "If you don't tell me what you know immediately, I might as well torture you."

Antoine licks his lips nervously, then decides he has no choice but to play out the hand and hope for the best.

"A trap was laid for your uncle and some others," he says. "The girl called Bec was the one they wanted, but your uncle and Beranabus were important to them too. Juni didn't reveal all the details, but from what I gathered, the trap was partially successful. Beranabus was killed, but the —"

"No!" Meera cries, taking a step in front of me. "Beranabus can't be dead."

"According to Juni, he is," Antoine says calmly.

"But —" Meera starts to exclaim.

"Leave it," I cut in. "If Beranabus is dead, he's dead. Let this worm finish telling us what he knows about Dervish."

Meera doesn't like it, but she pulls back.

"Bec and your uncle escaped," Antoine continues. "The attack took place at sea, on a giant cruiser. They got off before it sank and are adrift in a lifeboat. Juni was furious. When she calmed down, she told me to send a crew to intercept the lifeboat and finish the job. They have instructions to kill Dervish and bring Bec back alive. Taking no chances, I roused three separate units and dispatched them from different locations. The first should be upon your uncle —" He checks his watch. "— in sixteen minutes."

"Call them off," I hiss.

"I can't from here," he smirks. "But if you would kindly accompany me to my temporary office . . ."

I tremble with rage and hatred. If only I could rip the tongue from his mouth and swallow it whole — that would wipe the smirk from his face. But he has the upper hand, at least until I know that Dervish is safe. I'll have to allow him his smugness for a while. I start to agree to take him to his office, but Timas speaks before me.

"There's no need to relocate. I can see a radio unit in one of the boats. There are telephones and computer terminals set in the walls. We can communicate with the outside world from here."

"No," Antoine snaps. "There are things in my office that I need."

"Such as?" Timas asks with a little smile.

Antoine glowers. I see in his features that he had a plan in mind. The office was an excuse. He thought he could trick us and escape some other way.

"Don't play games," I say softly. "Your only hope is to prove that Dervish is alive and that we need you to protect him. If I think you're trying to weasel out, all bets are off and all promises are revoked."

"Come with me," Timas says commandingly, taking Antoine by the elbow and leading him to one side. "We'll work on it together. Tell me everything you did and how to undo it. I'll see to the rest."

"But . . . my equipment . . . ," Antoine says weakly.

"We have all the equipment we need," Timas says, taking a radio unit from a boat and fiddling with the dials.

With a bitter sigh, Antoine casts aside whatever plan he had in mind, sits beside Timas, and talks.

✠ The minutes pass quickly. Part of me is sure we'll be too late. Antoine's Lambs will have caught a strong wind and picked up Bec sooner than anticipated. Gunned Dervish down and dumped him in the sea for the fishes to feast on. I'm prepared for the worst and ready to rip Antoine to pieces when he breaks the bad news. My wolfen half is looking forward to that. It doesn't care about Dervish or anything except slaughter and feeding.

Dimly aware of Timas and Antoine talking on the radio, Antoine issuing codes and commands. Meera and Prae are listening in, but I'm too agitated to follow it all. I have very little patience since I changed.

Thinking about Juni's prediction again. I want to dismiss it. Me? Destroy the world? Ridiculous!

Except . . . it isn't. I've known since that night in the cave outside Carcery Vale that I have the power to annihilate not just a world, but a universe. Beranabus believed the Kah-Gash could be used against the Demonata, but it's a demonic weapon. Why should it work for us against those who created it?

I wish the contrary old magician was here. I need advice and guidance. But according to Antoine he's dead, killed on a ship, lost at sea. I should be in shock. I never liked the old buzzard, but he's protected this world for more than a thousand years and he's been my mentor for the last several months. His death should have hit me hard. But I only feel annoyed — why did he let himself fall into a trap now, of all times, when he was most needed?

"There we go," Antoine says, turning away from the radio. He salutes me with a sneer.

"What's the story?" I bark at Timas.

"We converted the assassination squad into a rescue crew," Timas says. "I was going to send Disciples, but it was simpler to use those already close to the scene. They've taken the survivors onboard and are flying back, but not to the city where Juni had arranged to meet them."

"Dervish?" I mutter, dreading the response.

"Alive," Timas says. "In bad shape — all three of them are — but breathing."

"Three?" Meera echoes.

"Dervish, Bec, and a Disciple called Kirilli Kovacs. You know him?" Meera shakes her head. "Apparently he was onboard when they went to the ship."

"What about Sharmila?" Meera asks.

"Dead," Timas says simply. "Along with Beranabus. Maybe Kernel too, but they weren't sure about that. A few thousand passengers and crew were murdered also."

"A good day's work," Meera snaps at Antoine.

"You can't blame me for what happened on the ship," he huffs. "I had nothing to do with that." He smiles thinly at me. "Those onboard the helicopter have orders to release the hostages only in *my* presence. A little insurance policy."

I stare at Antoine without blinking. "Dervish is safe?" I ask Timas.

"Yes."

"Then we're finished here."

I still haven't blinked. Antoine's fidgeting now.

"You haven't forgotten your promise, have you?" he laughs, trying but failing to sound lighthearted.

I shake my head slowly. And grin wolfishly.

"I assume you're a man of your word?" Antoine says stiffly.

"I'm not a man," I answer quietly. "But yes," I add as he turns an even paler shade of white beneath his tan. "I said I wouldn't kill you, and I won't."

Antoine breaks into a smile. All his confidence and arrogance come flooding back. He takes a step forward, eager to establish control of the situation. I raise a gnarled, semi-human hand to stop him.

"I said *I* wouldn't kill you," I repeat slowly. "But I said nothing about *them*." I gesture at the five werewolves.

Antoine laughs feebly. He thinks I'm joking. Then he looks deeper into my eyes and realizes I'm as serious as death.

"No!" he croaks. "You can't. Your uncle — they'll kill him if I'm not there."

"I'll take that chance," I chuckle, then click my tongue. Five pairs of wolfen ears prick to attention and the room fills with growls of grisly delight.

"Please," Antoine sobs, backing up. "I did what you asked. I cooperated."

I turn my back on him and nod at Meera, Timas, and Prae.

"Are you certain you want to do this?" Meera asks as the werewolves advance and Antoine whimpers and begs for mercy.

"Yes," I say flatly.

"It's a callous act," she warns. "This will stain your soul forever. You might regret it when —"

"When what?" I snap. "When I turn back into a human? When we defeat the Demonata and skip off into the sunset, holding hands? That isn't going to happen. This is what I am. Get used to it."

I step out of the room, feeling nothing but a dim sense of pleasure that Dervish is alive. "I don't think I have a soul any longer, if I ever had one to begin with," I tell Meera softly. "And my only regret is that there aren't more like Antoine to kill."

Then the air fills with Antoine's screams. I march ahead without looking back, smiling savagely as the scent of the traitor's blood reaches my nostrils. I lift my nose and breathe in deep. My eyes narrow. My mouth waters. My stomach growls.

Delicious.

LAST MAN STANDING

✠ ✠ ✠

I WANT to leave the island immediately, take a boat and sail for civilization, to be reunited with Dervish. But there are details to sort out first. As anxious as I am to press on, I don't want to leave a job half-done.

First, with Timas leading the way, we sweep the compound in search of any survivors. I'm not sure if I'd take them captive or kill them, but there aren't any, so that's a question that ultimately doesn't require answering. Werewolves howl gratefully as I pass. Their previous leader never treated them to anything like this. They think it's going to be like this all the time, dozens of soldiers to feast on every day. I'm sorry that I'll have to disappoint them. Maybe I can round up more of Antoine's collaborators and send them over — home delivery, Grubbs Grady style!

Once we're sure the compound's clean, Prae asks if I can move the werewolves out, so that she can re-establish the perimeter.

"Everything's changed," she sighs, running a hand through her grey hair. "We can't take them back — I won't subject them to slavery and experimentation again, not after this — but we can't just leave them here. They'd starve."

"I'm taking some with me," I tell her, and all three of them stare at me. "The attacks won't stop. Juni will send others against us. We'll have to fight again. And again. I'd rather do that with my pack than without them."

"But how will you control them?" Meera asks. "Off this island . . . in a city . . . you can't keep them like hounds."

"Yes, I can," I growl. "I'll have to treat them to a kill every so often, but that shouldn't be a problem, not with the sort of action I'm anticipating. I won't take them all, just the more advanced. Thirty, forty . . . no more than fifty."

"I don't think that's a good idea," Meera says.

"Too bad," I grunt. "Demons can't be killed by normal humans, but these have been tainted by the blood of the Demonata. They're creatures of magic. They can kill just about anything Lord Loss sends against us. So they're coming with me."

"What about the rest?" Prae asks before Meera can force an argument. "Will you move them out of the compound, so that I can restore the wall? I'll remain here and order supplies, do what I can to make their lives as pleasant as possible. This will be my new mission, putting right some of the many things I did wrong."

"You really think you can?" I frown. "Antoine wasn't working alone. The Lambs betrayed you. Are you sure you can make demands of them now?"

"I know most of those who sided with Antoine," Prae says, cheeks flushing with anger. "I'm sure I can expose the rest. I'll knock the Lambs back into shape. Remind everyone of our original mandate — to help those afflicted with the curse. We'll still search for a cure, but we won't breed or lie anymore. We won't even need to execute. We can offer an alternative now — this island."

"A holiday resort for werewolves?" I chuckle.

Prae smiles. "It sounds crazy, but why not? We couldn't do it before — they'd have ripped each other to pieces. But they've been altered. The modified creatures can control the others. We'll do the rest, feed them, guard them from the outside world, introduce new members into the fold as we reap them over the years."

I like the idea of a werewolf sanctuary. "OK. I'll give the order to retreat. You get to work on the walls. But Prae," I stop her as she turns. "If you don't treat them right, I'll come back. Understand?"

"My daughter's one of *them,*" Prae says tightly. "I'll treat them right." Then she leaves, Timas in close attendance to help her with the computers, while I howl and direct my pack towards the exits.

As the werewolves depart, I scan them for the strongest and smartest. I grunt at those I like the look of and hold them back. They willingly group behind me. They don't know what I want, but they trust me and wait as patiently as they can.

I gather thirty-seven in total. Large, muscular, spectacularly ugly beasts. The weirdest personal army in history, but they won't let me down. We'll kill demons together, as many as Lord Loss and the Shadow pit against us. Bathe in their blood. Grow fat on their flesh. Sharpen our fangs on their bones.

My wolfen troops put Shark's dirty dozen to shame. I smile wryly when I think about the ex-soldier. He would have appreciated the final push, the slaughter and blood-drenched victory. He'd have understood why I had to kill Horwitzer. Antoine was a worm who had to be squashed. Meera thinks I'm a monster for ordering his death, but Shark would have done the same. So would Beranabus and Dervish.

A year ago . . . hell, even a few hours ago, I wouldn't have. I was a child, with a naive sense of honor. Not anymore. We're fighting a war. The survival of the human race is at stake. Winning is all that matters. If we have to become kill-crazed beasts to defeat the demons, so be it. We don't have the luxury of guilt. Those of us who protect the world must place ourselves outside the morals of those we fight for.

When the last sated member of my pack crawls past, dragging a half-chewed leg, I give Prae and Timas the signal. They throw the relevant switches and the panels of the wall rumble back into place, sealing us off from the open spaces of Wolf Island. As the panels clang shut, my heart aches slightly. I want to be outside with the jubilant werewolves, running free. But I have obligations. My place lies away from this island.

"Come on," I growl at Meera and Timas. "Let's lower the boats and get the hell out of here."

"If you need help sorting out the Lambs, give me a call," Meera tells Prae. "I'll do whatever I can."

"Thank you." Prae smiles weakly. "I think I'll be able to handle matters myself, but I'll bear your offer in mind. Good luck with whatever you're heading off to do. I suspect our problems are minor compared to yours. I hope —"

"Wait!" I snap, stopping near the edge of the cliff. A few of the boats were torn to pieces by the werewolves while we were waiting for Timas to open the doors of the compound, but most are intact and secured in place. One, however, has been lowered, and a rope ladder dangles next to where it stood. Creeping forward, I glance over the edge and spot a figure below, bobbing about in a boat. It's a man. He's lying on his back, as if soaking up the sun.

"No way!" I roar.

"Who is it?" Meera shouts, but I don't stop to answer. Grabbing hold of the rope ladder, I throw myself from rung to rung. I'm dimly aware of Timas and Meera scrabbling after me, but most of my thoughts are focused on the man in the boat.

As I draw close to the last few rungs, I turn to study the figure. A dark mood descends. I'm convinced I was mistaken, that I only saw what I wanted to see. Or if it's really him, that he's dead. But when he half-raises a hand to salute weakly, I know that he's real and alive.

"Shark!" I yell, jumping into the boat and grinning with open joy.

"You look . . . weird," Shark wheezes, running a dubious eye over me.

"How?" I gasp. "The cave . . . the werewolves . . ."

"What?" the ex-soldier scowls as Meera and Timas climb

into the boat and stare at him like he's a ghost. "You don't think I can . . . take care of a few werewolves . . . by myself? "

"But . . ." Meera shakes her head, smiling slowly.

"I'd have been in trouble if . . . you hadn't swept the rest of the pack away," Shark mutters, sitting up, leaning forward and wincing. "But when I came out of the cave and found . . . the island deserted, it was simple to hobble over here and . . . lower a boat. I wanted to come and see what . . . was happening inside the compound, but that would've . . . been pushing my luck. Besides, I thought you might need to make . . . a quick getaway."

Shark's bleeding all over. His left ear has been bitten off. I can only barely see his right eye — it's a miracle he didn't lose it, as most of the flesh around it has been clawed away. He's missing the tops of all four fingers on his left hand, and the thumb and half his index finger on the right. As he leans further forward, I see a jagged hole in his lower back. Timas sees it too and bends over for a closer look.

"Some of your entrails are poking through," Timas says, reaching out to prod them back into place.

"Leave my guts alone," Shark growls, slapping the taller man's hand.

"You're a bloody wonder," I chuckle, then grab hold of the ladder. "Patch him up," I tell Meera and Timas. "I'll sort out extra boats for the werewolves."

"*Werewolves?*" Shark squints.

"We're taking some with us. I'm their leader now."

"I can't wait to hear about it," Shark says drily. "Just keep them well the hell . . . away from me."

"You're getting yellow in your old age," I grin, then shimmy up the ladder.

The last thing I hear, as I'm climbing out of earshot, is Shark asking Timas and Meera, "So, who's good with a needle and thread?"

TOODLE-PIPS

✠ ✠ ✠

I KEEP humming a tune to myself, one Dervish used to sing when he'd had a bit too much wine. "Speed, bonny boat, like a bird on the wing." But in my head I change it to, "Speed, bonny wolf."

I don't like boats. Too slow. We could have taken the helicopter that was on the island when we arrived — we'd have found the missing parts if we'd searched — but we couldn't have squeezed in all my werewolf buddies. Besides, I don't think Shark is in any state to play pilot. Timas and Meera patched up the worst of his wounds, but he looks dozy and keeps drifting in and out of consciousness, slumping over, then snapping awake when a wave hits the side of the boat.

Shark's with me and thirteen werewolves. He's covered in blood and smells like the juiciest steak in the world. I need to stay beside him to keep the werewolves in line or they'd fall on him and finish the job their brethren started.

Timas and Meera are in separate boats, a dozen werewolves to each. Meera's big-time edgy. Keeps checking over her shoulder to make sure the creatures aren't sneaking up. Timas, on the other hand, looks as content as any seafaring captain. He sings jaunty songs to his hairy, bemused passengers, and calls for them to join in the choruses. Apart from a few coincidental howls, he's not having much luck with that. I don't think there's going to be a choir of werewolves anytime soon.

"I don't like the way they're looking . . . at me," Shark mutters, a minute or so after regaining consciousness from his latest blackout. "Like I'm lunch."

"Don't worry," I tell him. "They've already had lunch. Dinner too. You'll be fine until dessert."

"Funny guy," Shark pants, then passes out again.

I check that Shark's OK, then focus on Timas in the boat ahead of me. He said he knows where he's going, that he's read lots of books about navigation. A while ago I might have been worried, but I trust the oddball now. If we were adrift in a snowstorm in Alaska, I'd follow Timas Brauss before I followed an Eskimo.

Timas guides us safely to dry land, and though we bump about a lot while docking, we come through unscathed. Unloading the werewolves, Timas looks pleased with himself, as he has every right to. An ambulance is waiting. We buckle Shark onto a gurney and roll him into the back of the vehicle. His eyelids flutter open as we're settling him in place. He looks around, scowls, and tries to get up.

"Easy," I say, pushing him down and tightening the straps around his chest.

"I'm not going anywhere," he barks. "I'm coming with you to . . . help Dervish."

"You're in no condition to fight," I chuckle.

"I don't care. I'm coming whether you . . . like it or not."

"I thought you said you were going to retire when we got off Wolf Island," Meera reminds him.

"I said I was going to *think* about it," he growls.

"Well, think some more on the way to the hospital," she snaps, and slams the door shut. His curses turn the air blue until the driver switches the siren on and hits the accelerator.

"I'm glad I won't be there when they finish operating on him," I note.

"Me too," Meera says, smiling at me. "How do you feel?"

"Hungry," I reply, then wink at her alarmed expression.

"You really believe you can control them?" Meera asks as we herd the werewolves into the waiting trucks, which will take us to the nearest airport and a specially chartered plane.

"Child's play," I smirk.

Timas is waiting for us at the trucks. He says nothing as I usher in the werewolves, standing by in case I need him. When the last door has been locked, he clears his throat. "I should keep watch over Shark. He'll want to return to action as soon as he's fit — probably before — and he's going to need help. I can do more for him than you."

"That's fine." I smile warmly and shake his hand, but lightly, aware that I could crack his fingers like twigs if I squeezed too hard. "Thanks, Timas. We wouldn't have made it off the island without you."

"I know," he says, then turns to Meera. "Time to make good on that promise."

"What promise?" Meera squints.

Timas grabs her and bends her backwards, supporting her with one arm. "A kiss for your sweet prince," he murmurs, smooching up to her.

Meera pretends to struggle, but then grins and treats him to a kiss that's even hotter than Shark's curses. It's an old style movie kiss, except with more slurping and tongue action.

"Break it up," I growl.

The pair come up for air, their faces red.

"That was nice," Timas gasps.

"Very," Meera agrees, and pecks his nose. "To be continued," she purrs, then turns from him with the natural grace of a model and sashays away.

"See you soon," I mutter.

"*Extremely* soon." Timas nods and hits the road, snapping his fingers like a hepcat.

✠ Meera's on her cell for most of the trip to the airport, deep in conversation with some of her fellow Disciples. Her face is creased with worry when she cuts the connection.

"Bad news?" I ask.

"There are reports of three potential crossings," she says. "All in major cities. The windows are due to open within the next forty-eight hours unless we can find the mages responsible and stop them."

"Three at the same time," I mutter. "Hardly coincidence."

"No," Meera snorts. "One's in the city where Dervish and Bec are."

"So Juni must already know that Antoine's troops failed."

"I hoped we'd have more time, but apparently not." Meera sighs. "I'll arrange to have them moved as soon as possible."

"No." My face is stone. "Let the demons come. I'll deal with them. It'll be a good opportunity to test my pack."

"Are you sure?" Meera frowns. "Juni and her masters want the pieces of the Kah-Gash. If you and Bec are in the same spot, they'll have a double shot at it. Maybe you should stay away from her until —"

"No," I growl. "No more running. They want a fight? I'll give them one they won't forget in a hurry."

"Juni beat you once," Meera reminds me.

"She won't again," I whisper. Not because I believe I can turn the tables on her, but because she doesn't want to. She needs me to destroy the universe.

"Grubbs?" Meera says softly. "Why didn't Juni finish you off?"

I don't answer. Thinking about what the mutant monster predicted. Wondering, not if it might be true, but rather how it will happen and when.

"Grubbs?" Meera says again.

I shake myself. "It doesn't matter. Are you coming?"

Meera sighs. "No. I want to, but I'm needed elsewhere. I can be of more use in the other cities, either help find the mages and kill them, or try to drive back the demons if they cross. I think we're all going to have to work very hard over the next few days to prevent a massacre that makes the losses on Wolf Island look like a drop in the ocean."

"I'll come when I can," I promise. "Tell the other Disciples that if they fail — if demons break through — I'll mop up. Once I've dealt with those coming to attack Dervish and Bec, I'll go wherever I'm needed and I'll bring my werewolves. We can fight them now. We don't need to be afraid."

"You idiot," Meera chuckles. "Of course we do." She hugs me tight, then stands on her toes, hauls my head down, and kisses my coarse, hairy cheek, ignoring the bits of human flesh caught between my fangs and the stench of blood on my breath.

She releases me and I draw back to my full height. Part of me wants to plead with her to come with me. We can pick up Dervish and Bec, then fly to a deserted island like the one we just left. An apocalypse is coming. It would be easier to sit it out, enjoy what time we have left and face the end with a resigned laugh.

But I'm Grubbs Grady. Magician. Werewolf. Kah-Gash. I don't do retreat.

"Give my love to Dervish," Meera sniffs, then leaves me to make my own way to the plane. The last I see of her, she's climbing into the front of an army Jeep, talking on her cell, looking lovelier than ever as she prepares to go to war.

With a self-mocking smile, I offer up a quick prayer to whatever gods might be listening. "If reincarnation is real, and I die soon, let me come back as Timas Brauss's lips!"

Then I head off in search of my half-dead uncle, hoping he doesn't croak before I have a chance to bid him goodbye.

THIS IS THE END, BEAUTIFUL FRIEND

✠ ✠ ✠

DERVISH refused to be admitted to a hospital. If demons attack him and Bec again, he doesn't want to be in a public building, where innocents might catch the crossfire. So the team set in place by the Disciples swiftly established a temporary medical base in a derelict building in a rundown part of the city where he, Bec, and the other survivor were taken.

Antoine Horwitzer's soldiers are waiting for me when I arrive. They line the corridor, heavily armed, exchanging dark glances with several troops in different uniforms who are working for the Disciples. The air bristles with tension when I walk in. The commanding officer of the Lambs' group steps forward and runs a cold eye over me.

"Where's Horwitzer?" he growls.

"Dead," I say bluntly.

"You killed him?" the officer snarls.

"No." I whistle, and the werewolves lurch into view. "They did."

The officer's face blanches. His men raise their weapons defensively. The other soldiers raise theirs too, even more alarmed than the Lambs.

"You have a choice," I say calmly. "Fight and die, or lower your arms and walk away. Horwitzer's reign is over. The Lambs are back under the thumb of Prae Athim. Surrender now and we'll call it even."

The officer licks his lips. "I'd want safe passage for my men," he mutters. "And I'll have to confirm it with —"

"No time for confirmations," I bark. "Drop your weapons and run, or stand, fight, and die."

The officer studies the slavering werewolves and comes to the smart conclusion. He lowers his gun and gives the order for his men to follow suit. I growl at the beasts behind me and they part, affording the humans safe passage. Once they've filed out of the building, I bring my werewolves in, line them up in the corridor, and ask to be escorted to Dervish's room. The soldiers are uneasy — I can smell their fear — but they do as I request. One takes me, while the rest remain, eyeing the werewolves anxiously.

I find Dervish relaxing on a bed in a large room, clothed in a T-shirt and jeans, no shoes or socks, hooked up to a drip and monitors, staring reflectively at the ceiling. Bec's in a chair nearby, head lowered, snoozing. She's also hooked up to a drip. In a bed farther over, another man, swathed in bandages, is sitting up and entertaining a gaggle of wide-eyed nurses. A couple of fingers on his left hand have been cut or bitten off, reminding me of Shark.

"— but I wasn't afraid of a few stinking zombies," the man — it must be Kirilli Kovacs — is saying dismissively. "I laid into them with magic and fried them where they stood. If there hadn't been so many, I'd have waltzed through unscathed, but there were thousands. They overwhelmed me, and the others too. It looked as if we were doomed but I didn't panic. I gathered Dervish and the girls and plowed a way through."

"You saved their lives," a nurse gasps.

"Pretty much," the man says with a falsely modest smile.

I clear my throat. Dervish looks over and beams at me. Bec's head bobs up and she studies my twisted body with a frown. Kirilli Kovacs scowls at me for interrupting, casts a sheepish glance at Dervish, then lowers his voice and continues his story.

"Sorry I didn't bring any chocolates," I tell Dervish, walking over to the bed and taking my uncle's hands. He squeezes tight. I squeeze back gently, not wanting to hurt him. He squints as he studies me.

"There's something different about you," he says.

"I've started styling my hair differently," I laugh.

"Oh. I thought it was that you were three feet taller, a hell of a lot broader, look like a werewolf, and are naked except for that bit of cloth around your waist. But you're right — it's the hair."

"There's something strange about yours too," I murmur,

staring at the six punk-like, purple-tipped, silver spikes that have appeared on his head since I last saw him. "The tips are a nice touch. Very anarchic."

We grin at each other. Dervish looks like death and I guess I don't look much better. We must make some pair.

"How's the heart?" I ask, letting go and taking a step back.

"Fine," he says.

"It's not," Bec disagrees. She stands, taking care not to dislodge the drip. "We heard about your transformation. Meera said you'd be bringing others with you."

"They're waiting outside. What about his heart?"

"I need a transplant," Dervish says. "Care to volunteer?"

"He needs to return to the demon universe," Bec says, ignoring Dervish's quip. "The doctors have done what they can, but if he stays here . . ." She shakes her head.

"Can you open a window?" I ask.

"Not right now. I'm not operating at full strength."

I formulate a quick plan. "Juni knows you're here. A window's being opened somewhere in the city. Demons will pour through. The air will fill with magic. I want you to tap into it, open a window of your own, and get him out of here."

"Don't I have any say in this?" Dervish asks.

"No."

My uncle chuckles, then lies back and smiles. "I won't go," he says.

"Take him somewhere safe," I tell Bec. "If I survive, I'll come —"

"You didn't hear me," Dervish interrupts. "I won't go."

"Of course you'll go," I snap. "You can't stay here. You'll die."

"So?"

"Don't," I snarl. "We haven't time for this self-sacrifice crap. You're hauling your rotten carcass out of here and that's that."

Dervish's smile doesn't dim. "I've been thinking about it since we were rescued. Do you know that Beranabus and Sharmila were killed?"

"Yeah," I mutter.

"We're not sure about Kernel," Dervish continues. "He disappeared. There was a lot of blood and scraps of flesh, but they mightn't have been his. Maybe he's dead, maybe not." Dervish shrugs, grimaces with pain, then relaxes again. "I want to choose my place and manner of death. Beranabus and Sharmila were lucky — they died quickly, on our own world. But they could have just as easily suffered for centuries at the hands of the Demonata and been butchered in that other universe, far from home and all they loved."

"Those are the risks we take," I say stiffly.

"Not me," Dervish replies. "I'm through. I served as best I could, and if this body had a bit more life in it, I'd carry on. But I'm not good for anything now. I'm tired. Ready for death. I'll fight when the demons attack, but if we repel them, I want to find a peaceful spot and give up the ghost in my own, natural time."

"Don't be —" I start to yell.

"Grubbs," he interrupts gently. "I think I've earned the right to choose how I die. Don't you?"

I stare at him, close to breaking. Dervish is all I have left in the world. I think of him as a father. The thought of losing him . . .

"I reckon I'll last a few months if fate looks on me kindly," Dervish says. "But that's as much as I dare hope for. My body's had enough. Time's up. The way I've pushed myself, the demons I've faced, the battles I've endured . . . I was lucky to last this long."

"But I need you," I half sob.

"No," he smiles. "The thought that you might was the one thing that could have tempted me to return to the universe of magic and struggle on. But you don't need anyone anymore. I saw it as soon as I looked at you. You've found your path, and it's a path you have to travel alone. Beranabus was the same. Kernel. Bec too."

He looks at Bec and winks. "Grubbs isn't the only one I'll be sorry to leave," he says, and the pale-faced, weary girl smiles at him warmly.

I think of things I could say to make him change his mind, but the horrible truth is, he's right. I can see death in his eyes. Every breath is an effort. He's not meant to continue. The afterlife is calling. It will be a relief for him when he goes.

Sighing, I sit on the bed and glare at the dying man. "If you think I'm going to start crying, and say things like 'I love you' — forget it!"

"Perish the thought," Dervish murmurs. "In your current

state, I'll be pleased if you don't start eating me before I'm dead."

"I'd never eat you. I have better taste."

We laugh. Bec stares at us uncertainly, then joins in. She sounds a bit like Bill-E when she laughs, and for a few happy moments it's as if me, my brother, and uncle are together again, relaxing in Dervish's study, sharing a joke, not a care in the world.

We spend the rest of the time chatting. Dervish and Bec bring me up to date on all that's happened since I left them at the hospital, locating Juni on a ship full of corpses, finding a lodestone in the hold, the Shadow using it to cross, Beranabus destroying the stone and expelling the Shadow but losing his life in the battle.

"He went heroically, in the best way," Bec says with a mournful smile. "He wouldn't have wanted to go quietly."

Then Bec tells me the Shadow's true identity. It's *Death*. Not a chess-playing, suave, sophisticated Death like in an old subtitled movie Dervish made me watch once. Or the sexy, compassionate, humorous Death in Bill-E's *Sandman* comics. This is a malevolent force. It hates all the living creatures of our universe and wants to cut us out of existence.

"How do we fight Death?" I ask. "Can we kill it?"

"I don't think so," Bec says.

"But it has a physical shape. If we destroy its body of shadows, maybe its mind will unravel. You said it didn't always have a brain?"

"From what I absorbed, its consciousness is relatively new." Bec nods.

"So if we rip it to pieces, maybe it'll go back to being whatever it was before?"

"Maybe." She doesn't sound convinced.

"I can be the inside man," Dervish says, only half joking. "Once Death claims me, I can work behind the lines and try to pass info back to you."

"Perhaps you could," I mutter. "Do you think it preserves everyone's soul, that the spiritual remains of all the dead are contained within that cloud of shadows?"

"No," Bec answers. "It's using souls now, but from what I understand, it wasn't always that way. It was simply a force before, like the blade of a guillotine — it ended life. Finito."

I scratch my bulging, distorted head. "This is too deep for me. I don't think I'll ask any more questions. I'll settle for killing or dismembering it."

"You believe that you can?" Bec sounds dubious.

"Of course." I stare at her. "Don't you?"

She shrugs, but says nothing. I see defeat in her expression. She thinks we've lost. She's convinced our number's up.

"Hey," I huff. "Don't forget, we're the Kah-Gash. We can take on anything. If Death was all-powerful, it wouldn't need the help of Lord Loss and his stooges. We can beat it. I'm sure we can."

I look from Bec to Dervish, then back at Bec again. "Remember what Beranabus preached? He thought the universe created champions to battle the forces of evil, that we weren't freaks of nature, but carefully chosen warriors. I used to think he was loco, but not anymore. Look at me."

I flex my bulging muscles and bare my fangs. "You can't tell me this is a fluke. I didn't turn into a werewolf by chance, when the chips were down. I was primed to transform. The universe gave me a power it knew we'd need. You probably have dormant powers too. We'll change if we have to. Adapt to deal with whatever we're up against. The Shadow doesn't stand a chance."

Bec looks at me skeptically. "What about Kernel? The universe didn't prepare him. He's dead."

"You don't know that," I contradict her. "Maybe he transformed like me and turned into a panel of light."

Bec giggles. I smile but it's forced. I feel like a hypocrite, offering her hope when Juni's prophecy is ringing in my head.

I start telling them about my experiences, Shark's dirty dozen, Timas Brauss, Antoine Horwitzer, the trip to the island. I'm about a third of the way through my story when Dervish's fingers twitch and he lifts his nose. A second later I catch the buzz of magic. A window has opened and the air's filling with magical energy.

"I'll tell you the rest later," I groan, getting to my feet and smiling lazily as magic seeps through my pores, charging me up.

"If there is a later," Dervish grunts, unhooking himself from the drip and the machines. He stands. A couple of the nurses with Kirilli Kovacs hurry over, scolding Dervish and demanding he get back into bed. "Peace!" he roars. "Demons are coming. Do you want me to lie here and let them slaughter you all?"

The nurses share a startled glance, then back off. Dervish wriggles his bare toes, checks that the tips of his spikes are stiff, then cocks an eyebrow at me. "Awaiting your orders, captain."

I prepare a cutting reply, then realize he's serious. He's looking to me to lead. That's a first. I've always followed, bouncing from my parents to Dervish to Beranabus to Shark. Now I'm being asked to make the decisions, issue the call to arms and lead others to their deaths. I should be unsure of myself, but I'm not. Dervish was right. I don't need a guardian anymore. I'm ready for leadership. More than that — I *want* to lead.

"We'll hit them hard," I growl. "We'll take the werewolves and soldiers. We don't know what they're going to send against us — demons, armed guards, maybe the Shadow itself. So we'll go prepared for anything."

I start for the door. Dervish and Bec trail close behind. In the bed across from Dervish's, one of the nurses says brightly, "Good luck!" But she's not saying it to us. She's saying it to Kirilli Kovacs.

I pause and look back. Kovacs is lying with his sheets pulled up to his throat. He looks like he's about to be sick. I think he was hoping we'd sweep out without noticing him, so he could pretend he didn't know we'd gone.

"Well?" I grunt, amused. Dervish told me a bit about Kovacs and his less than avid love of fighting, but even if he hadn't, I could have seen with one look that this guy's chicken, Disciple or not.

"Aren't you going, Kirilli?" a nurse asks, frowning.

"Of course I am," he puffs. "I just thought . . . I mean, I'm still recovering. . . ." He waves his injured hand at me, smiling shakily.

"I got up from my deathbed," Dervish murmurs. "Surely you aren't going to let a few missing fingers hold you back?"

"No!" Kovacs cries as the nurses glower accusingly. "I just meant . . ." His face darkens. He shoots me a look of pure spite, then recovers instantly. With a breezy smile, he turns to the nurses. "What I meant was, I have no desire to go to war in a dismal state of attire. I know my suit's a touch the worse for wear, but if you good ladies could fetch it for me, so that I might cut a dashing figure as I stride into battle to save the day . . ."

The nurses like that. They quickly bring Kovacs his suit, which turns out to be a natty, badly shredded stage magician's costume, with faded gold and silver stars stitched down the sides. But I must admit he wears the rags well. Pats dust away, tuts at the blood, then tips an imaginary hat to the nurses. "Later, ladies," he purrs. Then, to a murmur of approving coos, he slides ahead of me, flashes me a reassuring smile — as if I needed encouragement — and exits like a politician heading off to settle an important affair of state.

I bark at the werewolves in the corridor, leaving Dervish to round up the human troops. With a few simple grunts, I let the beasts know we're going to fight. They howl happily in response.

I'm excited as we step out of the building. I don't care what the enemy sends against us. According to Juni, I'm the worst threat to mankind in any universe. I've only myself to be afraid of, really.

Dervish, Bec, and Kirilli edge up behind me, backed by about fifty soldiers. Kirilli's teeth are chattering, but he stands his ground and lets magic gather in his hands. I don't plan to rely on him, but he might prove useful.

Bec looks more resigned than afraid. She's trying hard to believe we can win, not just this fight but all those still to come. But it's hard. In her heart she feels we're doomed. She'll give it her best, but she doesn't think we can triumph, not in the end, not against Death.

Dervish is smiling. He figures he's going to be dead soon, one way or another, so what does he have to worry about? He's picked his spot and chosen his fight. If he dies, it'll be on home turf. That's all that matters to him now.

The soldiers are nervous, though some hide it better than others. They know a bit about demons, that they can't kill the monsters, only slow them down. They're not in control of this situation, and I know how frustrating that can be. But the Disciples have chosen well. This lot will stand, fight, and die if they have to.

And they will.

I look around at my misshapen pack of werewolves and smile jaggedly. Of all those with me, these are the ones I'm counting on to cause the greatest upset. If our foes don't know about my lupine retinue, they're in for a nasty surprise. Demons are used to having it easy on this world. Most humans can't kill them, and they rarely have to face more than a couple of Disciples at a time. Thirty-seven savage werewolves are going to make for a very different experience!

I sniff the air. I hear horrified screams coming from several streets away. I'm eager to get into the action, but I delay the moment of attack, thinking about Juni's awful prophecy. Then, wiping it from my thoughts, I roar and let the werewolves break loose. As they race to confront the demons, I pound along in the middle of them. Dervish, Bec, Kirilli, and the soldiers lag behind. I'm grinning wolfishly, no longer worried about prophecies. Let the world end. Hell, let me be the one to end it! What does it matter? Nobody lives forever. If mankind's destined to bite the bullet, let's bite and be damned.

We turn a corner. I see hordes of demons running wild, humans fleeing the monstrous creatures. With an excited yelp, I lead my misshapen troops into action. As I zone in on the demonic army, I smile and think there's at least one guarantee I can make. If Juni's right, and it's my fate to destroy this planet, the poet got it wrong. The world won't end with a bang *or* a whimper. It'll end with the death screams of a thousand demons and a defiant, carefree, savage, wolfen howl.

The horrifying adventures continue in

DARK CALLING

Book 9 in THE DEMONATA series

Available now.

Turn the page for a sneak peek. . . .

A SMALL, wiry, scorpion-shaped demon with a semi-human face drives its stinger into my right eye. My eyeball pops and gooey streaks flood down my cheek. In complete agony, I scream helplessly, but worse is to come. The demon spits into the empty socket. At first I think it's just phlegm, but then dozens of tiny *things* start to wriggle in the space where my eye once swam. As I fill with confused horror, teeth or claws dig into the bone around my ruined eye. Whatever the mini-monsters are, they're trying to tunnel through to my brain.

Beranabus roars, *"Kernel!"* and tries to grab me, but I wheel away from him as insanity and pain claim me. I whip around, flailing, shrieking, wild. The demon strikes again and punctures my left eye. Darkness consumes me. I'm in hell.

A lifetime later, someone picks me up from where I've fallen and drags me forward. It might be Beranabus or Grubbs, or maybe it's Lord Loss. I don't know or care. All I can focus on is the blind hellish pain.

I pull away from the person or demon and run from the madness, but crash into something hard. I fall, moaning and screaming, but not crying — I no longer have eyes to weep with. The creatures that were spat into my eyes are muching on my brain now. I try to scrape them out with my fingers, but that just adds to the torment.

Then magic sears through my ruined sockets. The things in my head burn and drop away. The pain lessens. I sigh blissfully and slump.

✠ We return to the universe of the Demonata.

I'm stronger in the universe of magic. I numb the pain and set to work on building a new set of eyes. I'm not sure that I can. Magic varies from person to person. We all have different capabilities. Some can restore a missing limb or organ. Others can't. You never know until you try.

Thankfully I'm one of those who can. With only the slightest guidance from Beranabus I construct a pair of sparkling blue eyes. I build them from the rear of my sockets outwards, repairing severed nerve endings, linking them with the growing globes, letting the orbs expand to fill the gaps.

I keep my eyelids shut for a minute when the eyes are complete, afraid I won't be able to see anything when I open them. I hardly breathe, heart beating fast, contemplating a life of darkness, the worst punishment I can imagine.

Then Beranabus stamps on my foot. I yell and my eyes snap open. I turn on the magician angrily, raising a fist, but stop when I see his cunning smile. I *see* it.

"You looked like an idiot with your eyes shut," Bernabus grunts.

"You're a bully," I pout, then laugh with relief and hug him. He's laughing too but Grubbs isn't. The teenager glares at us. He's lost his brother and abandoned his uncle and home. He's in no mood to give a crap about my well-being. But that's fine. Right now I can't sympathize with him either. All I care about is that I can see. I relish my new eyes, drinking in the sights of the demon world.

I'm so happy, it's several hours before I realize I can see more than before, that my eyes have opened up to a wonder of the universe previously hidden to me.

✠ I've always been able to see patches of light that are invisible to everybody else. For years I thought they were products of my imagination, that I was slightly (*light*ly) crazy. Then I learned they were part of the realm of magic. I have a unique talent. I can manually slot the patches together and create windows between universes, far faster than anyone else.

I thought I might not be able to see the lights with my new eyes, but they work the same as my original pair. I can still see the multicolored patches, and when I think of a specific place, person or thing, some of the lights flash and I can slot them together to create a window. In fact, I can do it quicker than before, and my powers on Earth are greater than they were. Where I used to struggle to open windows to my own world, now I can do it swiftly and easily.

But now there are other lights. At first I thought they were illusionary specks, that my new eyes weren't working properly. But I soon realized the lights were real and fundamentally different from those I was familiar with. They're smaller, they change shape, and their colors mutate. The regular lights never alter in size or shade, but these new patches grow and subside, bleed from one color to another. A square pink panel can lengthen into a triangular blue patch, then gradually twist into an orange octagon, and so on.

They shimmer too. Their edges flicker like faulty fluorescent tubes. Sometimes creases run through them, like ripples spreading across the face of a pond.

I can't control the lights. They ignore me when I try to manipulate them. In fact, if I start to get close, they glide away from me.

There aren't many of them, no more than twenty or thirty anywhere I go. But they worry me. There's something deeply unsettling about them. I initially thought that I was nervous of them just because they were new. But several weeks later, as I was trying to coax them nearer and link them up, they whispered to me.

I know it's ridiculous. Lights can't whisper. But I swear I heard a voice calling to me. It sounded like static to begin with, but then it came into focus, a single word repeated over and over. It's the same word the lights have been whispering to me ever since, softly, shyly, seductively.

"Come . . ."

DARREN SHAN

THE THIN EXECUTIONER

THE EXECUTIONER SWUNG HIS AX –

THWACK!

– AND ANOTHER HEAD WENT ROLLING INTO THE DUST. THERE WAS A LOUD CHEER. RASHED RUM WAS THE GREATEST EXECUTIONER WADI HAD EVER SEEN.

When Jebel Rum sets out on an eight-month journey to petition the fire god for invincibility, he wants nothing more than to return and claim the post of executioner from his father. But the quest he and his slave embark on will set him off on the bloodiest fight of his life, and by the end of the journey, Tel Hesani is more than just a slave—he is Jebel's friend. Will Jebel sacrifice Tel Hesani to appease his brutal god, or will he find the strength to reject his violent upbringing to save his friend?

Inspired by *Adventures of Huckleberry Finn*, international best-selling master of horror Darren Shan injects this classic story with his trademark gore and breakneck speed, and champions the idea that peace is often the bravest choice of all.

CHAPTER ONE

The executioner swung his axe—*thwack!*—and another head went rolling into the dust. There was a loud cheer. Rashed Rum was the greatest executioner Wadi had ever seen, and he always drew a large crowd, even after thirty years.

Five executions were scheduled for that morning. Rashed had just finished off the third and was cleaning his blade. In the crowd his youngest son, Jebel, was more interested in the high maid, Debbat Alg, than his father.

To Jebel, Debbat Alg was the most beautiful girl in

Wadi. She was the same height as him, slim and curvy, with long legs, even longer hair, dazzling brown eyes, and teeth so white they might have been carved from shards of the moon. Her skin was a delicious dark brown color. She always wore a long dress, usually with a slit down the left to show off her legs. Her blouses were normally cropped and close-fitting, revealing much of her smooth stomach.

Rashed Rum tested his blade, then stepped forward. He nodded at the guards, and they led the fourth criminal—a female slave who'd struck her mistress—to the platform at the center of the square. Jebel slid up next to Debbat and her servant, Bastina.

"I bet she'll need two blows," he said.

Debbat shot him an icy glance. "Betting against your father?" she sniffed.

"No," Jebel said. "But I think she'll try to wriggle free. Slaves have no honor. They always squirm."

"Not this one," Debbat said. "She has spirit. But if you want to risk a bet..."

"I do," Jebel grinned.

"What stakes?" Debbat asked.

"A kiss?" It was out of Jebel's mouth before he knew he'd said it.

Debbat laughed. "I could have you whipped for suggesting that."

"You're just afraid you'd lose," Jebel retorted.

Debbat's eyes sparkled at the thought of having Jebel punished. But then she caught sight of J'An, Jebel's eldest brother, handing his father a drink. Debbat would have welcomed a kiss from J'An, and he knew it, but so far he'd shown no interest in her. Perhaps he thought he had no competition, that he could claim her in his own sweet time. It might be good to give him a little scare.

"Very well," Debbat said, startling both Jebel and Bastina. "A kiss if you win. If you lose, you have to kiss Bastina."

"Mistress!" Bastina objected.

"Be quiet, Bas!" snapped Debbat.

Bastina pouted, but she couldn't argue. She wasn't a slave, but she had pledged herself to serve the high family, so she had to obey Debbat's commands.

"Bet accepted," Jebel said happily. Bastina had a sour, pinched face, and her skin wasn't anywhere near as dark as Debbat's—her mother had come from a line of slaves from another country—but even if he lost and had to kiss her, it would be better than a whipping.

On the platform the female slave was motionless, her neck resting snugly in the curve of the executioner's block, hands tied behind her back. Her blouse and dress had been removed. She would leave this world as vulnerable as when she had entered it, as did everyone when they were executed. When the wise and merciless judges of the nation of Abu Aineh found you guilty of a crime, you were stripped of everything that had once defined who you were—your wealth, your clothing, your dignity, and finally your head.

Rashed Rum drank deeply. Refreshed, he wiped his hands on his knee-length bloodstained tunic, took hold of his long-handled axe, stepped up to the block, and laid the blade on the slave's neck to mark his spot. His eyes narrowed and he breathed softly. Then he drew the axe back and swept it around and down, cutting clean through the woman's neck.

The slave's head hit the base of the platform and bounced off into the crowd. The children nearest the front yelled with excitement and fought for the head, then fled with it, kicking it down the street. The heads of um Wadi or Um Aineh were treated with respect and buried along with their bodies, but slaves were worthless. Their bones were fed to dogs.

Debbat faced Jebel Rum and smiled smugly.

Jebel shrugged. "She must have frozen with fear."

"I hope *you* don't freeze when you kiss Bas," Debbat laughed.

Bastina was crying. It wasn't because she had to kiss Jebel—he wasn't *that* ugly. She always cried at executions. She had a soft heart, and her mother had told her many stories when she was growing up, of their ancestors and how they had suffered. Bastina couldn't think of these people as criminals who had no right to life anymore. She identified with them and always wondered about their families, how their husbands or wives might feel, how their children would survive without them.

"Come on, then," Jebel said, taking hold of the weeping girl's jaw and tilting her head back. He wiped away the worst of her tears, then quickly kissed her. She was still crying when he released her and he made a face. "I've never seen anyone else cry when a person's executed."

"It's horrible," Bastina moaned. "So brutal..."

"She was fairly judged," said Jebel. "She broke the law, so she can't complain."

Bastina shook her head but said nothing more. She knew that the woman had committed a crime, that a judge had heard the case against her and found her guilty. A slave had no automatic right to a hearing—her mistress could have killed her on the spot—but she had been afforded the ear of the courts and had been judged the same as a free Um Aineh. By all of their standards, it was legal and fair. Yet still Bastina shuddered when she thought about how the woman had died.

"Why aren't you muscular like your brothers?" Debbat asked out of the blue, squeezing Jebel's bony arm. "You're as thin as an Um Kheshabah."

"I'm a late developer," Jebel snapped, tearing his

arm free and flushing angrily. "J'Al was the same when he was my age, and J'An wasn't much bigger."

"Nonsense," Debbat snorted. "I remember what they looked like. You'll never be strong like them."

Jebel bristled, but the high maid had spoken truly. He was the runt of the Rum litter. His mother had died giving birth to him, which boded well for his future. Rashed Rum thought he had a tiny monster on his hands, one who would grow up to be a fierce warrior. But Jebel never lived up to his early promise. He'd always been shorter and skinnier than other boys his age.

"Jebel doesn't need to be big," Bastina said, sticking up for her friend—her mother had been his nurse, so they had grown up together. "He's clever. He's going to be a teacher or a judge."

"Shut up!" Jebel barked furiously. Abu Aineh was a nation where warriors were prized above all others. Very few boys dreamt of growing up to be a teacher.

"You'd be a good judge," Bastina said. "You wouldn't be cruel."

"Judges aren't cruel," said Debbat, rolling her eyes. "They simply punish the guilty. We'd be no better than the Um Safafaha without them."

"That's right," Jebel said. "Not that I'm going to become one," he added with a dark glare at Bastina. "I'm going to be a warrior. I'll fight for the high lord."

"You? One of my father's guards?" Debbat frowned. "You're too thin. Only the strongest um Wadi serve the high lord."

"You don't know anything about it," Jebel huffed. "You're just a girl. You—"

Rashed Rum stepped forward, and Jebel fell silent along with the rest of the crowd. The day's final criminal was led to the platform, an elderly man who had stolen food from a stall. He was an um Wadi, but he behaved like a slave, weeping and begging for mercy. He made Jebel feel ashamed. People booed, but Rashed Rum's expression didn't flicker. They were all the same to him, the brave and the cowardly, the high and the low, the just and the wicked. It wasn't an executioner's place to stand in judgment, just to cut off heads.

The elderly man's feet were tied together, but he still tried to jerk free of the executioner's block. In the end, J'An and J'Al had to hold him in place while their father took aim and cut off his head.

J'An would come of age in a year and join one of Wadi's regiments. When J'An left, their father would need a new assistant to help J'Al. The position should be offered to Jebel, but he doubted it would be. He was thin, so people thought he was weak. He hoped his father would give him a chance to prove himself, but he was prepared for disappointment.

Debbat turned to leave, and so did the other people in the square. But they all stopped short when Rashed Rum called out, "Your ears for a moment, please."

An excited murmur ran through the crowd—this was the first time in thirty years that Rashed Rum had spoken after an execution. He took off his black hooded mask and toyed with it shyly. Although he was a legendary executioner, he wasn't used to speaking in public. He coughed, then laughed. "I had the words clear in my head this morning, but now I've forgotten them!"

People chuckled, a couple clapped, then there was silence again. Rashed Rum continued. "I've been executioner for thirty years, and I reckon I've got maybe another ten in me if I stay on."

"Fifteen!" someone yelled.

"Twenty!"

The burly beheader smiled. "Maybe. But I don't want to push myself. A man should know when it is time to step aside."

There was a collective gasp. Jebel couldn't believe what he was hearing. There had been no talk of this at home, at least not in his presence.

"I've always hoped that one of my sons might follow in my footsteps," Rashed Rum went on. "J'An and J'Al are fine boys, two of the best in Wadi, and either would make a fine executioner."

As people nodded, Jebel felt like he was about to be sick. He knew he was the frail one in the family, not as worthy as his brothers, but to be snubbed by their father in public was a shame beyond that of a thousand whippings. He sneaked a quick look at Debbat Alg. She was fully focused on Rashed Rum, but he knew she would recall this later and mock him. All of his friends would.

"J'An will be a man in a year," Rashed Rum said, "and J'Al two years after that. If I carry on, they won't be able to fight for the chance to take my place." Only teenage boys could compete for the post of executioner. "I asked the high lord for his blessing last night, and he granted it. So I'm serving a year's notice. On this day in twelve months, I'll swing my axe for the final time. The winner of the mukhayret will then take my place as Wadi's executioner."

That was the end of Rashed Rum's speech. He withdrew, leaving the crowd to feverishly debate the announcement. Runners were swiftly dispatched to spread the news. Everyone in Wadi would know of it by sunset.

The post of executioner was prized above all others. The god of iron, Aiehn Asad, had personally chosen the first-ever executioner of Wadi hundreds of years ago, and every official beheader since then had stood second only to the high lord in the city, viewed by the masses as an ambassador of the gods. An executioner was guaranteed a place by his god's side in the afterlife, and as long as he didn't break any laws, nobody could replace him until he chose to step aside or died.

J'An and J'Al knew all of this, yet they remained on the platform, mopping up blood, acting as if this was an ordinary day. In a year the pair would stand against each other in the fierce tournament of the mukhayret and fight as rivals with the rest of the would-be executioners. If one of them triumphed, his life would be changed forever, and almost unlimited power would be his for the taking. But until then they were determined to carry on as normal, as their father had taught them.

Near the front of the crowd, Debbat Alg gazed at J'An and J'Al with calculating eyes. On the day of the mukhayret, the winner could choose any maid in Wadi to be his wife. More often than not, the new executioner selected a maid from the high family, to confirm his approval of the high lord, so it was likely that one of the brothers would choose her. She was trying to decide which she preferred the look of so that she could pick one to cheer for. J'An had a long, wide nose and thick lips that made many a maid's knees tremble. J'Al was sleeker, his hair cut tight to complement the shape of his head, with narrow but piercing eyes. The inside of J'An's right ear had been intricately tattooed, while J'Al wore a studded piece of wood through the flesh above his left eye. Both brothers were handsome and up to date with the latest fashions. It was going to be difficult to choose.

Beside Debbat, Bastina also stared at J'An and J'Al, but sadly. She was thinking of all the heads the new executioner would lop off, all the lives he'd take. The Rum brothers had been kind to her over the years. She didn't like to think of one of them with all that blood on his hands.

And beside Bastina, Jebel stared too. But he wasn't thinking of his brothers, the mukhayret tournament, or even Debbat Alg. He only had thoughts for his father's words, the horrible way he had been overlooked, and the dark cloud under which he must now live out the rest of his miserable, shameful years.